8 Dates of Christmas

Christmas

A Holiday Romance

Rielle Knight

Rielle Knight

Contents

Content Warnings

<u>Content Warnings</u>
Grief/loss
Cancer
Survivor's Guilt
Marijuana use
There are not a lot of spicy scenes in this book, but they are definitely NOT closed door.

Author's Note

No matter how fluffy my stories may be, there will always, and I mean **always**, be a layer of some fucked up shit in the character's backstory where I'm trying to heal part of myself from something. Apparently, this story is working on my unhealed grief and survivor's guilt.

I didn't know that this would be the first book of mine that the world would see. Yet, somehow, I think it was always meant to be this way. I was so focused on what I thought should happen instead of what God had for me. I hope you enjoy my metaphor of that on the pages that follow.

If you don't, *fa la la la la la*, that's not my business.

If you need content/trigger warnings, you'll find them in the prior section. If you like to go in blind, gone head and keep reading. Some shit is going to be funny, and some shit is going to be emotionally heavy. Blame the characters, not me. Being an author is much more of a spiritual experience than I thought it would be. I'm just the vessel through which this story was told. Thank you for giving my writing a chance, I hope you enjoy it.

Dedication

Initially, I had something funny and enticing, but that felt disingenuous after the words were actually on the pages, so boop. Backspace. Delete that. I got rid of it.

This is for everyone who's lost someone important in their lives, and now joy just doesn't quite hit the same, especially during the holidays. I want you to live like they're still here for you to make them proud. I hope that you feel a warm hug of reassurance from their spirit when things go wrong and a wave of joy when things go right.

Auntie Shawn. You always encouraged me to do something great, and I wish you were here to see it. Don't pay attention to the spicy scenes. It was an accident. :) I love you, and I miss you, and I pray that you continue to guide me to all of the places I can go. Most of all, I hope this makes you proud.

To my bro in law–Dwaine. I know your whole family misses you, but your little brother never stops honoring your life and memory even through his grief. Thirty years old was too young and I wish you got to meet your nieces.

Fuck Cancer.

Chapter 1

Kendrick

"You still coming to Frosty's with me or nah?" My brother, Khalil, is always up to some shit. He thinks we're contractually obligated to do everything together because we share a birthday.

Brushing my teeth, I play dumb, "Coming *where*?"

Groaning from the speaker fills my bathroom. I know exactly where he's talking about, but I can't resist the urge to fuck with him.

"Bro, why you always doin' me like this? You know damn well what I'm talking about. Frosty's, the Christmas bar downtown. Last year, I almost went home with three girls, but I had to go with Sherm, and he fucked it all up. Don't leave me hangin' again."

Emphasis on again. *He's not wrong.* I'm not the most reliable partier, and I will dip quicker than my cousin Ray whenever a girl says, 'I'm pregnant' if something doesn't feel right, or if I get tired, or if I get hungry. Honestly, I'm dippin' at the slightest inconvenience. Add in the fact that it's a Christmas gathering, and I'm doubly sure I don't want to go.

"What's in this for me?" I ask, rinsing my mouth.

A video call request comes through, and I accept it, knowing he's going to be annoyed. Khalil isn't even trying to hide his disbelief. "Women, duh! Or are you finally admitting you're—"

"Finish that sentence, and I'll remind you that you're the one always getting—"

"Aye aye, cut that shit out. You know I can't help that my face is prettier than yours."

"We're identical, fool. If I come, what time should I be there?" I close the remaining buttons on my shirt, dropping my gaze so he can't see me holding in laughter.

"Ain't no if you come and nine." Raising a hand in front of his camera he says, "Don't start bringing up nine is late. I know it is, but we don't want the ladies on the prowl for marriage."

"Aight Khalil, I'll see you later." I know I've stunned him by not arguing, but it's been a while since a woman has graced my bed, and if they want holiday dick, I can help with that. I haven't been in an actual relationship since the she-devil, and I'm damn sure not finding her at a *Christmas* bar. I wish it would be January already so people can stop cosplaying like they're saints or something because they volunteer during the holiday season.

With my laptop bag in hand, I head to the elevator. My apartment's tiny—barely bigger than the size of a crayon box compared to my old place—but it's within walking distance of my job. On the base floor of the building is a coffee shop. It's not the best I've ever had, but it's decent. Plus, I'm supporting a small black-owned business, so I try to go every morning.

The bell jingles, and I roll my eyes at the gaudy Christmas decorations when I enter. The barista greets me with her signature flirty smile.

"Hey, Kendrick." Her voice is laced with an exaggerated sultriness, but I'm tired of reminding her that she's too young for me, so I ignore it. Sure, I'm only thirty-five, but there is a world of difference in our ten-year gap.

"Morning, can I get a—"

"Large hot with honey and oat milk." She fills in correctly. Closing off the steaming cup of coffee, she manages to make the act of sliding on a heat sleeve look oddly seductive. *I didn't know it was even possible.*

"I've got you right here." Her breasts spill out of her shirt as she leans to pass my liquid energy, and I try my hardest to keep my eyes up.

Once I have a good hold on the overly festive Christmas cup, I hand her money, including a couple extra dollars for a tip, and then head out. The walk to my building is short, and the coffee warms my ungloved hands despite the December chill biting at my fingertips. While I'm typically the picture of responsibility, I always forget gloves. I need some of those clip-on things my little sister Kaliyah puts on her kids' coats.

Pushing the rotating entrance of the One North building, I swipe my badge and breathe deeply, putting on my corporate face before walking into the office.

Christmas music blares through the office speakers, so I pop in my earbuds as I sit down to drown out the noise, noise, noise. The only holiday music I want to hear is *Merry Nothin'* by Jessie Reyez, and even that's a stretch. Agreeing to go to this bar must mean I'm lonely if I'm going to voluntarily suffer listening to that one song at least a dozen times. I shiver thinking about it when my phone vibrates on my desk.

Khalil: REMINDER

Khalil: 9 pm- Frosty's up north. Don't act like you forgot. I'll bring the hat.

If he thinks I'm wearing a Santa hat, he's lost his mind.

Me: I fucking dare you

Khalil: LOL I'm already knowing bruh... It's a Grinch hat. *smirk emoji*

A smile touches my lips as I think that maybe tonight might be the fun I've been needing, but it quickly drops when I notice the meeting with Haverly, that wasn't there last night. I glance at my watch and see it starts in...fifteen minutes. *Great.*

"Hey, boss." Marshall, my assistant and developer in training, peeks through the cracked door.

"If it's about the meeting, I saw it pop through."

"Oh, ok, good. That's what I was coming to tell you. Haverly emailed me some docs to print for you. AAI wants to make more changes, and I don't think you'll like it."

With a grimace, I grab the stack of papers from him. *I'm so fucking tired of this company.* Unlimited edits are included in the higher tiers, but come the fuck on, man. *When's it going to stop?* This is beyond ridiculous. Honestly, it's Lanada. Even her assistant, Shanice, agrees, and her hints of being over the whole thing make me laugh.

Our banter started after an accidental response a few months ago when I typed out my actual thoughts on the design. I thought I was going to get fired for sure, but her response was, "Me too." Since then, she has sent a follow-up with her sarcastic thoughts with every update. Marshall prints and deletes them so we don't mistakenly respond to the wrong thread.

Since I'm about to meet with Haverly, I don't bother reading the design changes; instead, I see what Shanice has to say about it.

From: ShaniceJ@AAI.web
To: Kendrick.Thompson@Chi.WebDesign.com
Subject: Sorry
Mr. Thompson,
I just forwarded yet another list of revisions. I know the list is extensive (again), and I'm sure you're thrilled to dive into another round of "minor tweaks" that somehow turn into full-scale projects.

I know that last update wasn't well-received because the colors "didn't feel quite right" (whatever that means), so please make sure to work your magic and channel the inner visions of someone who can't articulate what they want.

No rush, though. Except it's urgent because everything always is. Thanks for your patience – seriously, you have more of it these days than I do.

Best,

Shanice D. Jones

Design Assistant to Lanada Hamers

Artisan Aesthetics Interiors

"May you never be too grown up to search the skies on Christmas Eve." -Anonymous

My nose wrinkles when I read the festive signature. Grabbing my laptop and a notebook, I head to the conference room. Inside, Haverly has the video ready, alongside a tray of breakfast snacks.

"Let's skip the small chat. I'm done being lenient with AAI. I have other projects for you to lead, and you can't do that if this one is tying you down. Plus, today marks six months."

Well shit, that's unexpected, but welcome. "I'm happy you agree. I won't be able to get to the Henderson project if this one is still in development. I should be in third phase of editing by now."

"I'm aware. They're going to join in a few. Let me handle the discussion."

"Got ya." Though I didn't see this coming, it brings a glimmer of relief. Legs crossed under the table, I sit back and wait for them to pop onto the screen. *It's beyond the time to call this a wrap.* I only hope that Shanice gets on camera today so I can see her before this project ends.

Chapter 2

Shanice

"Shay, you promised!" My best friend, Kennedy, doesn't shy away from the dramatics.

"How long do I have to stay?"

Exasperated, she slides back into the camera. Should I be on the phone with my bestie at work? Probably not, but it helps the day go by faster.

"We're going to a bar, not getting a kidney removed."

"It's basically the same thing," I mutter. "I don't know, my mood just isn't there today."

"I'm not letting you sit in the house. Your mom wouldn't want you wallowing around."

Points are being made. Mom *wouldn't* want me wallowing around, focusing on the fact that she's gone, but she's gone so it's not like she can yell at me. Since I'm at work, I shy away from the thought process. I wanted to take today off, but after I sent those requests to Chi Web Design yesterday, my boss from hell canceled my PTO. Lanada's going to be *really* pissed when I give notice tomorrow.

"I can't talk about Mom right now, please. And there will be men at the bar. You're not the one who swore off men."

"Hell nah, I didn't swear off men, and I'm not going to. You're delulu as fuck. It's been six months… You tryna end up a cat lady like your neighbor down the street?"

"If it means I'm not swapping dick, I'll take the cats. My battery-operated boyfriend is safer than any of these men out here."

"Bye."

I'm not being dramatic about this. Six months of my life went down the drain when I caught my ex on the phone with his fucking wife. *Men really ain't shit.*

"Don't bye me, heifer. What kind of bar is this?"

Giddy, she shimmies her shoulders, "It's the Christmas bar downtown. One of my coworkers went the other day, and they said the men were men-ning. I need that."

"They were probably also mar-ried."

Scoffing, she responds, "Bitch, don't put your trauma on me. Look... It happened. You were fucking the brains out of a married man for months, but you *didn't know* he was married. There's a difference. Now you know to look for finger tan lines and watch to see if they're texting late at night. My friend—"

"What friend?" I hate when she casually drops in that she has friends other than me.

"Unh unh... Don't get territorial now when you were the one—never mind. ADHD brain. Anyway, my friend did a reverse search of this cropped picture this dude sent her, and he cut his wife out of it. Dumbass."

My computer pings, and an email from Ted Dancir, the CEO, comes through with the subject "Time to talk?" Aw hell, did they find my emails to Kendrick? *I'm about to get fired.*

I don't get the chance to read it because knocking on my office door means I'm about to be dragged into some bullshit. Whispering, I hold the phone up to my mouth, "Gotta go, text me." Disconnecting the video call, I tuck my phone into my drawer.

Cruella with a bad wig, also known as Lanada, opens the door without waiting for my response. "I need you in this meeting. The developers are probably going to push back on a rework of the website."

There's no Hey, how are you? How you doing—she just jumps right in. I'm not surprised to hear they're pushing back because I would, too. She's changed the plan six times already. They really should have fired us as a client a long time ago, and I've not so subtly told the web designer in charge the same thing.

Laptop in tow, I follow behind her. I'm off-camera since she prefers to treat me as someone neither seen nor heard. I've never been in a meeting with the developers, though. My communication has been purely via email. The Collab meeting opens, and I notice the woman first. I'm not sure who she is, but *damn*, is that Kendrick? He's fine as fuck— brown-skinned with a nice beard and broad shoulders. If his teeth are pretty, I might melt right here.

"How you doing, Lanada?" His velvety voice greets her, and I catch the subtle shift she makes in her seat. *Nasty.*

Smoothing her tone into something too polished to be natural, she replies, "I'm great Kendrick, thanks for asking. Haverly, you set this meeting, so I'll let you start." *Apparently, she knows how to give a proper greeting after all.*

Haverly is one of the higher-ups, but I could be wrong. She's an older black lady, but her flawless appearance reminds me why I take collagen every day. "Hello Lanada, I'm happy to hear you're doing well, but I have some concerns. Let's get right to it. I've had a chance to review the email from your assistant and the requested changes, which combine elements of designs one and two that Kendrick has already prepared. While we offer unlimited changes, another design re-do is not in our scope of capabilities. I would like to point you to section 16.2A on the contract, which states that developmental changes are limited to six months of building, and I'm afraid we have reached that marker. Within the terms, it says if we cannot come to an amicable design, we have the authority to terminate the contract."

Internally, I wince because I know it's there since I pointed it out to the attorneys. Lanada looks at me to confirm what was said, and I nod. This whole mess is her fault–her endless nitpicking and indecisiveness. Not one to explode in front of someone else, she begins typing notes rapid fire on her computer.

Sitting forward, Haverly pulls up some designs on the screens. "Let's continue."

I take notes as she talks because they're great ideas, but that is why she is the boss. I have to admit that it looks very similar to the design she just turned down, minus a couple of color changes and box placements, but I won't mention that. She'll feel swindled. Once the meeting closes, her fake smile drops, and I know I'm in trouble.

With an icy tone, she asks, "How could you have missed that term?"

Huh? "I didn't miss anything. After the attorneys reviewed the contract, I flagged it in your calendar months ago. I assumed we would be done by now."

"Well, you're fired."

Say what? "Uh... I think I misheard you."

"You heard me. I said you're fired. Do not expect a letter of recommendation." She must have messaged HR while we were in the meeting because Susan's bug head ass comes strolling in, closing the door behind her.

This bitch has got to be out of her mind. "You're firing me for something that isn't *actually* my job... Do you realize how insane that is? Let's not forget it violates the terms of my contract."

"And now you're insulting me?!"

"You just told me I was fired and wouldn't get a recommendation. What the fuck do I have to be nice for? You were the one more interested in looking at the developer than you were in actually completing this project. If anyone should be mad, it's Ted because this could have been done months ago."

"Can you have her escorted from the building?"

"No need. My box has been packed for weeks."

Lanada is more than petty— she's reckless. Susan hands me forms and review them. After signing, I ask, "Susan, can you follow me to my desk? I don't feel safe alone with her."

Susan looks back and forth between us like she has no clue what's happening right now. "Um, sure. Yeah, sure I can."

What I like about this firm is working up close and personal with some of the industry's best interior designers. What I hate most about this firm is working up close and personal with my boss. She's mediocre at best. I realized early on she does a lot of skating while holding onto the coattails of others. Some people are great at what they do, and some are great delegators. I think that's why she's been in this position as long as she has, but today is the last day I ever have to listen to her rant. *Hallelujah for that.*

As I'm getting walked out, Ted blocks the walkway between my desk and the exit. Arms crossed, he asks, "What's happening here?"

Hands clasped in front of her, Lanada raises her chin. "Shanice has been terminated."

"Why?"

"She was going to resign anyway, but she missed a critical term on the contract for the company that was supposed to be handling our website revamp."

"Is she one of the attorneys that we pay to review our contracts?"

"No, but—"

"She's not an attorney, nor is she a personal assistant. She's a design assistant, right?"

Lanada fists her hands at her side like a pissed off toddler, but he's right. This isn't the job I was hired for.

"Yes, but—

"Are you trying to get us sued for wrongful termination?"

"No, but—"

He interrupts her attempts at excuses by asking, "Shanice, may I have a word with you, please? Susan, I'll take those papers. You can go back to your office."

I ask, "Is this including Lanada as well?" Her chin tilts high in the air, and she takes a step forward, but he raises a hand to stop her.

"I think this would be best with you and me—alone. Lanada, you told me this firm was expensive because they're efficient and do an excellent job, but it's been six months. I'll put a meeting on your calendar to discuss your handling of this project separately."

She folds into herself from the weight of his words and sulks off.

Turning his back, he walks to the elevator so we can go up a floor to his office. I scurry behind him. His private elevator is in the back corner, so when he comes down to our floor, he has a great view of what's happening, but that means everyone can see me walking behind him—and usually—that means a bad day for somebody. As I'm trailing him, I feel burning stares on my back. The swoosh of the elevator doors closing feels like doom as we're lifted to his floor. Usually, I enjoy peace and quiet, but right now, the silence is chilling. His receptionist, Jenna, smiles warmly as we enter. Instead of going into his office, we go to a seating area off to the side.

"So you were going to resign—can you tell me why?"

"Well..." It's awkward to explain to the CEO that one of his head designers is horrible. Maybe I can just talk about the job itself. "My role is not what I thought it would be. Don't get me wrong, I know I'm very efficient when it comes to task management and organization, but my role has been more of a personal assistant than a design assistant. I know I've been helpful, but I want to do what I thought I was hired to do. Working here was a dream come true when I got the position, but it's not what I imagined it to be."

He looks at me like he's trying to find the words I'm not saying. Crossing his hands on his lap, he sits forward. "So, you're not doing the job that you were hired for. Do you have another position lined up already?"

"Uh, no. I just…" My words trail off, and I sigh. I already got fired; it's not like this is going to get me in any more trouble. "I can be a personal assistant anywhere, and if that's the best job for me, I would rather do it somewhere that's less stressful."

"Do you think you could do Lanada's job better than her?"

Whoa… I never said that. "Sir, that's not what I was trying to say, I just want to be an interior designer."

"Relax, Shanice. Did you read my email this morning yet?"

"Sorry, I didn't get the chance to because I got pulled into that meeting."

"There's no reason to apologize. I asked you if you had time to talk about another opportunity within the company. I'd like to offer you a new job, Shanice. How would you like to be a junior designer?"

My mouth is practically touching the floor. "Sir, are you sure about that?"

"While *you* don't think that you've been a design assistant, I've watched the notes you've added to each of the projects that come across my desk. Every contract has been positively affected by your input, so I would like to give you the chance to take more control. It would also mean you work on this floor and report to me."

"But only senior designers are up here."

With a chuckle, he responds, "I was planning on giving you a different office on that floor, but since Lanada just tried to fire you, I think an exception would be necessary."

"Is the offer now or never?"

"Unfortunately, I need an answer on this sooner than later because we were scheduled to post at the end of the day. That's why I wanted to speak with you before you left today." Jenna brings over a piece of paper and hands it to me. "These are the terms. I'm going to eat an early lunch, and when I get back, I hope to have an answer from you. You don't have to stick around. Just check in with Jenna before you leave." Drumming his hands, he smiles and nods once more before he gets up and walks away.

What the hell am I supposed to do now? Staring at the form, I bite my lip and read. It's twenty-five thousand dollars more than I make now, and I still get bonuses, plus I can work remotely once a week. In a situation like this, it's too good to be true, but I do what anyone else would... I sign my name on the dotted line. *This is going to change my life.* Tonight, it's time to celebrate.

Chapter 3

Kendrick

Khalil: Aye you on your way? I said 9pm foo

Me: Ever heard of fashionably late?

Khalil: Not when I'm here by myself bro. Bring ya ass or I'ma scoop all the ladies for myself.

Parking my pickup on the side street, I grab my coat from the passenger seat and slide it over my shoulders. Winter in the Chi is hit or miss. Last year, it was fifty degrees, and there wasn't a lick of snow in sight. It's a cool thirty tonight, so I make sure to button up.

From the outside, it doesn't look like much, but I googled this shit before I came, and I have lots of concerns. The line is long as fuck, and everyone looks so... festive... *Could this be any cheesier?* I pull out my phone so they can scan the ticket Lil sent me, then walk down the entry created with walls of greenhouse plastic and pvc piping. The quickly moving line changes to a standstill wall of bodies clogged near the red balloon arch. I peer around and see the holdup is from folks stopping to take pictures with a nutcracker. Huffing, I walk around the swath to cut through the line, and *oh...my...God.*

I'm going to kill him. I'll literally remove his entire soul from his body, because what the *fuck* is this? I can barely move a few feet in front of me. The pictures showed three floors sparsely filled. This mother fucker is packed to the brim. While I'm not claustrophobic, I do not like germs, and this is a cesspool. Walking sideways, I get in where I fit in. There's a corner by the bar that has a little free space, and I make that my destination before texting my brother.

> Me: Are you fuckin for real Khalil?

> Khalil: Yo! You made it? Where you at? I'll come scoop you.

> Me: What the hell is this man? Where are you? You ain't tell me it was gonna be packed like this.

> Khalil: FYM, I said it gets busy in this bitch and that's why we're here late.

> Me: *No*, you said we were coming later to avoid the mamas looking for their kid's new stepdaddy.

> Khalil: Oh ok, my bad. Where you at tho?

> Me: I'm in the corner of the bar on the main floor.

> Khalil: aight bet.

A few minutes pass of me staring unbelieving at the massive crowd. Shit like this is why that virus is still a thing.

> Khalil: Actually, it's a little tight getting up the stairs. Can you come down to the basement bar? I'll have a drink ready for you.

I need a blunt, not a drink. Two women entering catch my eye, and my coat slips from my hand. The attendant catches it, but I look like an asshole now. While I wait for my ticket, I turn back to find them laughing and snapping pictures. They're both gorgeous, but the taller one's smile takes my breath away. And that catsuit—*Damn.* Since it takes five minutes to go about three hundred feet in this mess, I lose her in the crowd, but it's my mission to not leave without her.

Changing directions, I head back to the basement. Some girl offers me a necklace that looks like a rope of Christmas lights, but over my dead body would I be caught wearing that. Walking sideways—because there are three lines of people scrambling down the stairs—a guy sideswipes me from behind. I'm very comfortable with my sexuality, but that doesn't mean I want a dick rubbing against me. *Pause.* Internally, I want to scream like an overstimulated toddler. Once I reach the bar, I nudge my twin with my shoulder.

"Damn, there's two of you?" Shorty next to him looks back and forth between us. Sticking her chest out, she bites her lip and slightly moans, which is weird as fuck. "I always wanted to have fun with twins."

That was the wrong thing to say. It's not that we haven't fucked the same girl because shit, life happens. We don't have any sexual encounters together, though.

"You done fucked up." Khalil says, placing his fingers against her forehead and moving her out of our way. He passes my drink and nods to this roped off section. Over his shoulder he says, "We don't do threesomes *together*, that's nasty."

Not that we mean to knock someone else's kink, but nah. We've shared everything since the womb—but sex—and it will stay that way until we die. Back in high school a girl used him to try to get to me. It hurt him a lot more than he lets on, but we made a bunch of rules after that. He's a very successful architect, so it's dumb as fuck to compare him to me. Meanwhile, I wish I could tap into some of his charisma.

Though I wouldn't consider this real VIP, the section we enter is better than the floor. Snowflakes and oversized ornaments fill the ceiling space above us. Someone thought it'd be funny to display tiny elf toys in compromising positions. They're giving fellatio, taking it from the back, and riding cowgirl... Well, I do like that position a lot... Vigorously shaking my head, I move past the thought that will have me hard as fuck in here like a damn creeper, but I snap a few pictures to laugh at later. I have to admit, that's funny as hell.

I take a sip from the drink included with the tickets, and I'm immediately disgusted. I promise I'm not a liquor snob, but this tastes like it's contaminated with well water. Somebody's cutting the liquor and doing it horribly. Choking, I spit the drink back into the cup and put it down on the floor near me.

"Damn, you can't finish a bar drink. Wannabe whiskey-sommelier face ass." Shaking his head, Khalil continues, "I know it's overcharged and shitty, but in my experience, a bad drink ain't never stopped me from having a good time." I don't miss the shiver when he chugs the last of his cup. He sticks out his tongue and grimaces—like that's gonna help.

"Alright, you got me. I'm a 'lil more bougie, but that's just me being a grown man and not wanting to settle. I ain't got no shame in my game."

Rolling his eyes, he changes the subject, "When I checked it out earlier, most of the women in groups were on the main floor. Down here it's a lot of dicks and the couples, the singles stick around the top floor."

"Did you take a canvas of a bar for the most likely to be fucked pussy?"

"I'm thirty-five, too. I gotta be efficient in this muhfucka."

We look at each other for a moment before bursting into laughter. He's annoying as hell, but I love my brother. Somebody is going to knock him on his ass one day, and he's going to fall fast and hard, but I can't wait to see that shit. Lowkey, I think he's looking. I'm actively looking for my forever, but she's got to be right. Being in a position to finally be a provider, not just financially but also physically and emotionally, I'm definitely ready to sit my ass down somewhere, but tonight's about fun.

When he stands, I do the same, dusting my hands on my pants and gazing around the room. While there's no way I'll find my forever in this place, as soon as I do, I'm never letting go. For now, I need some company to warm my bed. If I have my way, she's tall, with browned-butter skin, a beautiful smile, and a giant mane of curls. I just have to find her.

Chapter 4

Shanice

"That's the sixth hard dick to rub against me, I'm feeling *very* violated here, Kennedy."

Rolling my eyes, I grab the second disgusting drink. This time, I told the bartender not to water it down further with ice. I'm going to take this back like a shot. They cut the alcohol with well water and there is a bitterness that makes it undrinkable. I pinch my nose and chug it down. My nose crinkles and the left side of my body twitches a little bit. Is it dramatic? *Possibly.* Is it warranted? *One thousand percent.*

Kennedy tips her empty glass to mine and says, "That's nasty as fuck, but we don't waste no drinks out here, *okay?!*"

"Damn straight. What kinda man you lookin' for tonight? You going daddy or father?"

She looks around the ever-growing crowd and then pulls her bottom lip between her teeth. It will be a cold day in hell before Kennedy trusts another man, but I don't blame her after what happened.

"I'm thinking father. I ain't had this cat beat up by an older man in a while. What about you?"

"Honestly, I'm just here to people watch and distract myself. The drinks were supposed to be a celebration, but they're horrible, so there's that."

Her head snaps back, and she turns to face me. "The fuck you mean you're here to people watch? I hope you mean you hoping to watch someone flick your clit cuz ain't no damn way you leaving here alone tonight. Not after all this effort we put into your outfit."

I'm wearing what I can only describe as a catsuit with this top that said Mrs. Claus on the tag, but there's no way Santa was leaving the workshop if this is the kind of outfit she was tinkering in. It's basically glued to me and there's going to be nothing sexy about peeling this off. "Girl, whatever. It's clothes. Clothes ain't gonna hide my mood. It's been a weird day."

"Bitch, you got a promotion *after* you got fired. That's a sign to think anything is possible tonight, not to think about every way this could go wrong."

With a sigh, I deflate a little in my seat. "I can't help it. Sorry, that's my default."

Nudging her shoulder into mine, she assures me, "Self-deprivation is a lot of people's go-to method to talk themselves out of stuff. Just know I'm not standing or sitting for that shit."

"Okay, I can promise to try. I just don't have— "

"If you say something stupid like I just don't have high hopes, I will turn this bitch into an auction for your bed." Holding her finger up like a scolding teacher, she has me pegged, and not in the way I like it.

"Alright, alright. We're going to the top floor actually to mingle."

I jump when she smacks my ass hard enough to sting. With a follow-up squeeze, she says, "That's my girl."

"You nasty." This is how we always are. Both handsy and, most of the time, we get mistaken for lesbian lovers, but that's a no from either of us. As a bi-sexual woman, people seem to think I can't have friends that I'm not attracted to, but she's like my sister. She *is* fine as hell, though.

"Please Lord, let me find somebody to match my freak tonight." She pretends to pray until I smack her hands apart.

"You goin' to hell for that," I laugh, "but Amen."

In a fit of giggles, we scoot toward the upper-level stairs. We collect our final pre-paid drink with the ticket at the bar. When we first arrived, they gave us a shot, which was far more enjoyable than the rest of the well liquor.

For the final drink in our package, I pick the strongest one on the menu, at least by what the bartender claims. It still tastes dirty, but it'll do. Though the drink tastes like ass, I tip the bartender and stroll toward the front. We didn't buy a section because we didn't know how it would be, so I'm happy to find a clear corner in here. *It's a lot of fucking people.*

"Aye, you see him over there?"

"Him who? It's a lot of hims in here."

Smacking her lips, she twists my head into the sea of men. "Don't be stupid girl, the only me worth looking at! He over by the bar with that Santa hat on and the sexy ass wide shoulders."

Is that... Oh shit, it's Kendrick she's talking about. "Oh yeah, he's fine. Gone head and put him in your coochie pocket. If that's the same person, I think he works for Chi Web Design."

Her eyes bug out, "I know you fuckin' lyin'. The one you've basically been crushing on via e-mail. You said his voice alone got your panties wet. No, you go talk to him."

"Abso-fuckin'-lutely not. *And* I do not have a crush on him. It was just friendly banter."

Arms crossed, she leans against the wall. "I didn't know commiserating about your stupid ass manager with the client and *risking your job* was friendly banter but go off. Plus, he don't know you from Peter, you were never on the screen so just make up a fake name, fuck his brains out and send him on his way. Since you got a promotion, you're not even going to talk to him anymore. You better go sit on that man's face!"

"No, you go talk to him. Plus, you saw him first, dibs matters."

"Girl, he's a person, not a parking space. You can't call dibs on a person."

"That's not what you said about Rodney."

"Bitch, that was middle school. After everything you've been through, you deserve to have some fun. Don't let Dickless control your life. You're worth a thousand of him."

Cutting her eyes over to me, she waits, but I stay in place. While I appreciate her concern for my dating life, I just don't have it in me to be hurt again.

Since I don't give her a response, she says, "Fuck it, I'll just tell him to come over here. You said his name is Kendrick, right?"

"Yup." I pop the p for emphasis because I would know that face anywhere. *It only took one time of seeing him to etch his features into my mind permanently.* On the screen, he exuded a quiet confidence, the effortless kind that turns heads. Even though he wasn't looking at me, there was a magnetic pull in his intense gaze and his voice—it's low and smooth, and I bet my money that he could talk me through it.

"Alright, bet. If his name is Kendrick, I'm bringing him this way. If his name ain't Kendrick, he's mine."

"I'll be waiting." I lie, but I'm pretty sure she already knows that. When she points back to me, I'll be gone, and she'll be forced to cover for herself and pretend it was a joke. This game is well-practiced, and she falls for it every time.

I stroll leisurely around the floor. Sure, the decorations are on the excessive side, but they liven the whole place up. Laughter bubbles out of me as I come upon two naughty elves. After snapping a picture, I think of sending a photo to Mom, and then my heart falls to my feet. *Mom.*

If there was anything Vanessa Jones loved, it was Christmas. It breaks my heart that she'll never see this place. The snowflakes, the elves, the randomly dangling tinsel, and the lights' festivity would make her holiday. Not that I don't enjoy Kennedy's company—because that's my bestie—but if Mom was here, we would be taking pictures and thinking of some funny things we could add to our own decor. Last year, I couldn't celebrate without her. Now that I have to maintain her legacy, I'm going all out. A line of beautifully painted nutcrackers come into view, and a little empty space surrounds them. I decide this will be my new relaxation spot, and then I head that way.

Navigating through the crowd isn't my favorite part of the evening, but it's live in here. While hiding, I hear a velvety, yet somehow also familiar, voice say, "If they play this shit one more time, I'm going to lose it."

Only one song has been on a five song cycle since I've been here. His complaint makes me laugh and I say, "Bet you they play it again within fifteen minutes."

His throaty chuckle makes me rub my knees together. "There's no way I'd make that wager because they might play it even before that."

"How many times you heard it?"

"Shit, about four. I was trying to ignore it, but my brother left me to go get some shitty drinks from the bar."

"Oh my gosh, I'm glad it wasn't just me and my friend. I had to choke that last one down." My laugh ends awkwardly when I notice his sudden silence. "Sorry, that was too much, huh?" I don't really know what I said wrong, but I can't see his face since there is a median between us. Annoyed with myself for making things weird, I shake my head. *Way to go Shanice, way to go.*

Chapter 5

Kendrick

Clearing my throat, I try to focus as the blood rushes back to my brain. It's been way too long since I've been fucked if hearing her say 'choke that last one down' made my shit brick like this.

"Nah, it wasn't too much at all. My brain just went elsewhere." I was too busy imagining peeling that skin-tight outfit off her, right after I tear off that God awful Santa vest.

"Oh, you nasty." She laughs from the depth of her soul, and the sound is music to my heart.

"Why you hiding out in the back looking like that?"

"Oh, you peeped what I look like, huh? I ain't even see anybody over here."

"I'm probably here for the same reason you are. Your sibling brought you as a wing person?"

"Oh no, my best friend conned me into this. I love Christmas."

"For a second there, I almost thought you could be my person, but you love Christmas. I hate this shit."

Scoffing, she asks, "What do you mean you don't like Christmas? That's blasphemous."

"It's blasphemous because I don't want to be bombarded by the requirement to spend hella money, or go into debt so I can prove I love people I see only around the holidays when they want something? *That's wild.*"

Silence rolls over us, and I think until she speaks. *Did I come off too strong?* I want to smack myself because Khalil told me before we split ways not to talk about how much I hate Christmas. He reiterated it would ruin my shot, and here I go rattling off an elevator pitch. Where is he anyway, it doesn't take this long to get two drinks. He must have found a woman for real. I'm happy as fuck I drove myself because I don't want to bother with trying to find a ride share in this crowd.

"Well, I was wrong," her voice pierces through the silence between us. "It was only four songs."

I take a step closer to the edge of the nutcrackers between us. Only about three feet separate us, and her soft and dense curls are the first thing in my view. With the little glimpse of personality I've seen...I think I've found the one—for the evening.

Curious, I ask, "Would you ditch your friend?"

I watch her lean her head against the chest of the Nutcracker. Biting her lip, she holds her words back from me.

"Don't get quiet on me now. Use your words, Sweets."

She's quick to respond this time. "I'm not getting quiet, just thinking."

I'm on my toes, waiting for the rest of her response because her energy is enamoring.

"As intriguing as you are, *whoever you are*, I made a promise to myself, so I'm gonna have to pass. That's not a dig on you, but I'm not looking for a man right now. Serious or unserious. This was a fun conversation, though."

Well, that sucks. "I get it. I wish that *wasn't* the case, but I get it. Can I... Can I at least meet you officially?" I move back a little just in case she turns this way and wait.

"Who the hell do you think I am?" She laughs and turns the corner. I finally see her big brown eyes. Dots of gold dance in her irises before they widen. Her head whips over to the bar, confusion replacing the gorgeous smile on her face.

Her lips are tight as she stares at my face and clothing like something doesn't match.

"Everything okay?" I ask after a very long silence. *Is something wrong with my outfit?* I know I'm kind of casual but some of these people have horrendous outfits on, at least I'm stylish. Snatching off the stupid Grinch hat she keeps looking at, I get insecure for probably the first time.

Forcefully, she shakes her head like she has to snap out of it. "Sorry, I saw someone who looked exactly like you at the bar with a Santa hat, and my friend just went to talk to him. I didn't mean to be weird about it. I'm Shanice."

Everything clicks into place now. "You had me out here thinking I disappointed you or something," I chuckle. "Yeah, that's my twin brother, Khalil."

"You're identical?"

"Down to our toes." Her brows furrow and I want to smack myself. *Why the fuck would I say down to our toes like we stand around measuring dicks?* Something about her has me off my game. I talk to beautiful women all the time, but something about her energy calls to me.

"My bad, that was weird. I meant, yes, we're identical. I'm Kendrick."

She freezes up, like that was the wrong thing to say. Becoming ever more awkward, this is no longer a pleasant exchange. She's fine and all, but this is weird.

"Actually, ya know… I'ma head out. I keep freaking you out, and I promise I'm not always this off my game."

I get no more than three steps away before her hand touches my arm. "Sorry, I think I need to be transparent. I work for AAI."

AAI… Why does that name sound—Oh. "You work for Lanada, wait…*Shanice*?! As in email Shanice? Lanada's assistant, Shanice?"

She cringes, "The one and only. I'm sorry if I stopped your fun, but I had to explain what was happening, so I didn't look like a creep."

"Nah, I 'preciate that because I definitely thought something was wrong with me, but I can't believe it's you. You wanna get a drink or something?"

Disgusted, she says, "I would rather drink flat pop for a month, plus mixing business just doesn't seem like a good idea."

"I'm happy you don't want another because I don't know how I could look like a strong man drinking that. We've been exchanging emails for months. Don't run away from me now. It's like meeting a pen pal in person."

"You're too much." Her phone ringing in her pocket interrupts her laughter, but she struggles to open it.

"New phone?"

"Unfortunately, I know these phones are super cool and all but changing from a different system confuses me."

"May I help you?" I extend a hand and wait for her to hand it over. It takes a minute for her to let me help but one she does I show her the message from her friend.

Bestie: He's not Kendrick. Where you at? He's trying to take me where his brother is but I'm not tryna leave you hanging.

She sends back a quick message that she's with me—Kendrick—and to meet us by the wall of nutcrackers. I'm reading over her shoulder and was hoping she would say something more interesting, but she doesn't.

We spend a few minutes setting everything up, including her wallet and face ID, and then I walk her around most of the standard features. If she didn't know I was a technology nerd before this, she *definitely* knows now. "Only one thing left to do."

Lifting her brow, she says, "And that is?"

"Take the first selfie." I'm looking straight at the camera, and she has her head tilted in my direction, smiling brightly with her hand on my arm. *It's perfect.* Clicking on the share button, I tap airdrop and send it to myself.

"You're way too smooth with this."

Close to her ear, I whisper, "Baby, you should see what happens when we aren't in a crowd full of people."

Breathy, she says, "Too bad that can't happen."

"And why the hell not?"

"You hate Christmas, so we could never work. That's a non-negotiable for me. Plus, the work connection makes it weird."

She's got me there but Christmas being a non-negotiable is wild. I've never had someone not want to be my friend because of my holiday stance.

"Alright, alright. I get it. But for real though, I enjoyed hanging out with you tonight. Can we at least be friends?"

"Not 'can we be friends'... I thought you were better than that."

"I mean, I am. You cool people and we have been kinda a little bit friends for a while now, we just didn't meet each other in person. Maybe you can help me find a Grinch version of you to become my wife."

She's quiet for a while before she acquiesces. "I can do friends, but I mean it. Don't text me talking about benefits unless you want to be redirected to human resources."

"Oh, you takin' these job analogies to heart, I've got you."

"How do I save your number?"

Deciding I want to show off a little, I place my phone under hers and select "share contact information" when it pops up on both phones.

"That was cool, but how do I turn that off?"

"I can't teach you everything, Beautiful."

"Okay whatever. I guess anyone who taps my phone will be able to get my number then since you don't wanna—"

Pulling her phone back into my hands, I go to settings and turn off sharing because fuck that. When I look up, she's smiling conspiratorially, and I realize I've been played.

"Smart woman."

Her smile is bright as she twists from side to side. "Only on days that end with y."

I can't stop the rumble of laughter from falling out. "You're too cute for your own good, you know that?"

"Sometimes."

I twitch as a loud voice permeates our little bubble. "Would you look at what we have here?"

A feisty looking light-skinned girl walks up with my brother. Where Shanice is tall, I'd say five-nine, her friend is about five-five and what the girls would call slim-thick. Interestingly, we're attracted to friends who look more like sisters. If Shanice didn't like Christmas, she'd be perfect, but perfect doesn't exist.

Chapter 6

Shanice

In my ear, Kennedy whispers, "Damn girl, there's two of 'em. I kinda want to meet their daddy... for research purposes."

Covering my mouth with my hand, I shake my head. "You are something else, you know that?"

"I mean, duh, but I said I was tryna hit up a father. I wonder if he's single."

Kendrick and Khalil have a short exchange over to the side before they turn back to us, and I'm stunned by the resemblance. At this point in life fraternal twins are a dime a dozen, but these men are identically *fine*. God bless their mama and daddy.

"Ladies..." Khalil says, smiling at us both. They even sound alike—this is dangerous. "There's a bar up the street that doesn't have shitty drinks and more than five inches of space for dancing. You in?"

"As much as I don't wanna be a party pooper, I'm exhausted, and I have to work in the morning," I say.

Clearly disappointed, Kendrick objects, "Tomorrow is Saturday. Can't you stay out a little longer?"

"I know, but we can't let our nine-to-five stop us from fulfilling our dreams."

Kennedy raises a hand to high-five, and I meet her in the middle. She follows with, "I know that's right, baby. I can take you home. I don't want you to get a cab from here. That's a waste of money."

Stepping forward, Kendrick says, "I can take her if she doesn't mind if that's the only way for me to steal a few minutes with her. My brother will probably pout all night if I pull you away from him so quickly. Plus, she's right. I have a project I should get to early in the morning, too."

I missed the point where I asked him to take me home. After having an overprotective big brother who did way more than I wanted growing up, I get triggered by his statement. "I can get a car. It's not a big deal, honestly. Nice to meet you, Kendrick and Khalil." Kissing her cheek, I wave goodbye to the guys and walk toward the door.

"Text me when you get home." She calls to my retreating back.

"Okay, Mom," I call over my shoulder. I trip step because I've said that phrase a million times, but surrounded by her favorite things, my heart squeezes. Now that I know how to use this phone, I take some pictures and videos along the way for inspiration. Taking the long route to the coat check, I bask in the Christmas joy. Outside the doors, Kendrick is standing near the curb wearing a long black overcoat, looking up and down the street. He's smacking himself on the forehead like he's scolding himself.

Walking behind him, I say, "You didn't miss me."

He jumps and then snaps his head to the side. "Damn girl, I ain't know you was a ninja."

Holding up the only karate arms I know, I laugh and then back up. "I said I can catch a cab. What you doing out here?"

"I'm not tryin' to be forward, but I—umm..."

The chemistry between us is on fire, and I know that if I step in, I'll be consumed by the flames. "I really think it's best if I go home—alone."

"No, that's not it. Can I take you home? I promise I'm not trying to be forward, just to give you a ride. I would call my mama to vouch for me, but she would do the same for my brother, and we both know that's not the case. My pops would kick my ass if he knew I let one of my friends pay for a ride when my vehicle works just fine."

"Seeing how my best friend is with him, that probably wasn't the best thing to say." I laugh so he knows I'm not serious. She keeps a mousekatool on her at all times, so I'm not concerned with my bestie. At the same time, I don't really want to take a cab, and technically, we have been communicating for months, *fuck it.*

"You should call for your car then." He blinks hard when I pull up my camera and snap a photo of his face. The flash brightens the night, and he looks like a deer in headlights. Opening a group text to Dad, Bestie, and Twelve, I send the picture of him. My brother Spencer—aka Twelve—is a Chicago cop, and I won't let him forget it.

> Me: If I go missing this is who did it.

> 12: The hell?

> Dad: What is going on, Shanice? Why would you go missing?

> Bestie: ahahahaha

> Dad: Why is that something to laugh at, Kennedy?

A video call vibrates in my hand. Twelve is displayed on the screen.

"Damn, you got twelve boyfriends? That's why you don't wanna add no more?"

Rolling my eyes, I turn and answer the call. "Wassup, bro?"

Kendrick hears the greeting and starts walking. "I parked over here; I didn't get valet."

"Don't wassup bro me. What kind of message is that to text? Have you lost your entire fucking mind?"

I love my brother to life, but he does too much and apparently doesn't know how to take a joke. Before he even became a cop, he was playing super save his little sister. I appreciate it, but I'm thirty-five, not sixteen.

"Oh, don't get your po' po' panties up in a bunch. It was a joke. I'm about to get dropped off at home by a new friend. It was one of those serious but not serious moments."

His nostrils flare on screen. "That's not a funny fucking joke. What the hell do you mean you're getting a ride from a *new* friend? Don't talk to strangers was the first lesson we learned as kids. Share your location with me, now!" He hollers.

"Yo, I understand you're her brother, but you ain't gotta talk to her like that," Kendrick says into the phone screen, glaring at my brother. I didn't know he walked back toward me, so I jumped from the force of his voice into my ear.

Unimpressed, Spencer says, "I assume that was you in the picture?"

"Kendrick L. Thompson. Because I see you care about your sister, I'ma show her how to share her location with you, but I'ma also show her how to turn it off because she deserves privacy, and you seem like the type to overstep the line." Stepping back, he gets out of the camera to let me continue the call.

Trying to lighten the mood, I say, "I'll send it to you, and for real, it was a joke. Apparently, it was just not a good one."

Sighing, Spencer pinches the bridge of his nose. "I'll call your father. Don't do that anymore, please. You know both of us are going to go into detective mode."

"Dad was a private investigator. You're the only cop around here, Donut Boy."

"Huuuuh you're annoying. Night, sis."

"Love you."

"Yeah, yeah. Love you too. Don't forget to send me your location."

Rolling his eyes, Kendrick grabs my phone before I can respond, clicks a bunch of buttons, returns to the camera, says, "Done," and then hangs up the call.

"I know that went far out of bounds. I'm sorry. I shouldn't have said or done any of that."

It was very forward of him, but I'd be lying if I didn't say my panties are sticky from how sexy it was to watch my brother get knocked down a peg. Usually, men are turned off when I tell them my brother is a cop—especially black men—but it's understandable.

"Where's your car?"

Shocked, he blinks a few times, then extends an arm down the block. "I'm parked over here. Since you're almost as tall as me I think you'll appreciate the space."

"Are you... are you in the pickup truck?" My words turn into a squeal as I realize what vehicle he has.

"That's me."

"You have an F-450? Are you kiddin' me?" Taking quicker steps, I walk up to my dream pickup and graze my hand against the grill. This mother fucker is sexy. I don't know much about cars, but I saw this one in a car show on a date with my ex and fell in love.

"Not that I think women are dumb with cars, but I've never seen a woman get so excited over a pickup truck unless I was offering to haul something for her."

"Let me drive it!" My excitement is palpable until I see how quickly his face falls, and he shakes his head no, vehemently. Muttering, I say, "Never mind then, I guess."

"Nobody drives Roxie."

My nose crinkles at the name. It's honestly a basic bitch name. She needs something more special. Snapping a picture of his license plate, I add that to that group chat, then take in her Chrome details. "I'ma call her Shantel."

"How the hell you just gone rename my car?"

"Like I just did. Come on and open Shantel up so I can slide up in her."

The engine purrs like my cat is right now, and I hold onto the door handle as the rumbling vibration skates across my body.

"Where am I going, lollipop?"

"What am I? The stripper from *Friday After Next*?"

"Where am I going, woman?"

"I live in Morgan Park. Go to the Sports Center, and I'll tell you how to get there."

"Damn, you really not telling me your address, huh?"

He's managed to get every bit of information he's desired from me tonight. It's better this way, *just in case*. I direct him down the proper streets to get to my house while avoiding conversation with music, but he's humming along, and I can only imagine the... *Jesus. Focus hoe, focus.*

"I'm on the left up here." I damn near missed my house.

With a soft peck on the cheek, I hop out of the truck and open the gate through to the rear property. "Thanks for the ride!"

I hang up my coat inside my townhouse and turn on the shower to wash off the evening. Thankfully, it doesn't take long for it to warm, and before I can complain the scalding water is beating against my skin. Meeting Kendrick in person was something I never thought would happen, but he's so much more domineering than I could have imagined. Thinking about his soft touches and the depth of his voice makes my hands glide over my body. Pulling the showerhead from the arm, I flip the rain head to the jet and imagine his tongue instead of the spray of water pressing against my clit. When pleasure rolls over me, I sit back on the shower bench and ride out the waves.

Still feeling unsatisfied, I walk naked into my bedroom, crawl onto my king-sized bed, and grab Winston from the drawer. There is absolutely no prep needed because I'm leaking from making myself come once already. Swirling in circles, I exhale as the girth of it fills me. I got swiped by six dicks tonight, but none of them were the one I actually wanted to feel—and also stupidly denied. Rolling my hips, I hold Winston in place and rock against it. Clicking on the remote, I buck on the bed as the vibration starts at low speed.

Continuing my pace, I roll onto my stomach while the pressure and suction automatically increase. Goosebumps travel over my body, and I scream into the comforter from the intensity as I picture him beneath me, grabbing my hips to encourage deeper strokes. Biting at the fabric, a feral moan leaves my mouth until I'm run ragged from the pressure of pleasure. If just being in the presence of that man makes me go home and fuck myself until I blackout, *I think I gotta block him.*

Chapter 7

Kendrick

Khalil: Aye, shorty nasty and I think I might be in love.

Me: bragging already, are we?

Khalil: Ain't my fault you don't know how to pick 'em right. Last night was the most fun I've had all month, bro.

Khalil: Thanks for coming, that was really fun.

Me: I know how to pick women perfectly fine. Shanice is just a friend.

Khalil: This the same Shanice you randomly bring up in conversation because of shit she says in emails?

I don't bring her up that much, do I? Maybe I do here and there, but... nah, he's fucking with me. Before I can call his bluff, he texts back about Kennedy again.

Khalil: Well, y'all can keep talkin in emails if you want to but I'ma marry Kennedy. Just as soon as I convince her to give me her number.

Me: ahahaha she ain't give you her number? I might not have gotten ass last night, but I got this.

Scrolling through my contacts list, I snap a screenshot of her contact card. Using the marker function, I black out her number but leave the picture to brag.

Khalil: Oh, you took a selfie, *how cute*. BUT you also got a dry dick soooo who really won?

Leaving him on read, I scroll over to the message function and risk it. I've had her number for less than twenty-four hours, and I'm already out here simping. What can I say that doesn't sound like I'm only trying to fuck?

Me: Morning, beautiful. I'm just making sure you're up working on your dreams.

The message is read pretty quickly. Three dots appear, and then—nothing. Damn, maybe I should have included a thirst trap. Deciding not to dwell, I set my phone aside and opened my laptop. Her advice from last night sticks with me: *Don't let your nine-to-five stop you from working on your dreams.* On weekends, I focus on projects that feed my soul, like developing websites for nonprofits. It's all pro bono, but the work feels good. Just as I get into a groove, my phone buzzes. I snatch it up, but it's not Shanice.

Sis: Wyd today?

Me: Not babysitting...

Sis: Come on Kendrick! I need help here.

Me: Is there a reason you didn't ask your parents? I'm working on a project right now. I literally just turned on my computer.

Sis: *Side eye emoji* Now you know your parents don't stay home on the weekend.

Sis: Khalil left me on read, and I promise I came to you last because you always end up being the one to help me, but I really need you.

Sis: It's another job interview. It will help me change to the daytime when they're at school.

I lay back on my couch and groan, then suck up my pride and help my sister. It's not that I mind helping, but why do I always have to be the responsible one? It's not her fault her husband passed away, so I don't hold it against her, but I really wanted to have a relaxing weekend. Setting my goals aside, I pick up my phone to say yes because if she can switch over to regular hours, it means less babysitting for me. Not that I don't wholly adore my nieces but *fuck*. A message comes through with a video of the twins pouting saying, "Pretty please, Uncle Cheese," and just like that, my hard exterior melts, despite their use of this lame-ass nickname.

Me: If they stop calling me uncle cheese I'll do it.

Sis: Done! We'll be there in ten minutes.

Sis: You're a lifesaver. I love you most :)

Me: Yeah, yeah love you too.

Her twins are fraternal, Luna looks like Kaliyah and Leah looks more like Desmond. It's a gift and a curse. Work is set aside, and my laptop is locked away. Inside the back of my closet is a large tote with toys, books, and coloring supplies. They're seven, so they're slightly independent if they have stuff to do, but sometimes they coerce me into taking them places.

The doorbell rings. She wasn't joking when she said she was only ten minutes away. The girls come rushing through without stopping to hug me and run straight to their bin.

She smiles graciously and says, "I'll be back in about three hours max if that's okay. After this interview, I need to shop, and it's easier…"

Without the kids is the unsaid part, but I can handle three hours.

"Got it. Good luck, for real. I hope it all works out."

She kisses my cheek, hugs the girls, and then rushes off.

"Alright, tiny monsters, what are we doing today?"

"Uncle Cheese, can we go to the park?"

Sick of this nickname, I cross my arms. I don't even know where they got that name from, but they've been calling me that since they could talk. "I thought we said no more, Uncle Cheese. Uncle Kenny."

"Uncle Kenny, can we go to the park?" They repeat in unison while jumping up and down.

"Alright, I guess we can go. Leave your coats on. It's cold outside."

After several minutes of fighting over which toy they wanted to hold, we left my apartment. My area is nicer than where we grew up, but I'm still cautious whenever I take the girls out with me. I had to get hit by a mail truck while riding my bike for my family to get the leg up we needed. I've made incredible investments and have more money than I know what to do with, but I'm scared that one day I'll make some mistake, and it'll all be taken from me.

I'm smacking myself for not bringing the wagon when I have to lug the girls back home. They're definitely capable of walking, but having to slow down to a tiny human pace is annoying. Our only detour is this winter market because I don't feel like enduring the argument. I let them pick one thing to leave at my house as our little secret, but that's why my toy bin is so full now. I'm a sucker when it comes to them.

Kaliyah knows I spoil them, but that's my job as their uncle, and really, it's all she allows. She's turned me down whenever I've offered to help her, except for watching the kids. Finally, back in my apartment, my phone vibrates in my pocket as soon as I get my shoes off.

> **Sis:** you're going to hate me.

> **Me:** Tell me something new

> **Sis:** I went shopping crazy. Can you bring the girls home?

> **Me:** You're right. I'm really not fond of you right now.

> **Me:** *toddler throwing a tantrum gif*

> **Sis:** I love you too

She's lucky I love her. I slide my shoes back on and look in the closet for the spare booster seats. *Looks like we're taking the Subaru.* The girls chatter away in the backseat when we get stuck by a freight train, my mind drifting back to Shanice. The memory of her laugh, confidence, and energy is all I can think about.

I pull up the picture we took at the bar and can't help staring at her.

"Uncle Kenny, who's that?" Leah asks, leaning over my shoulder.

"No one," I say quickly, locking my phone. "Sit back in your booster. The train's almost done."

But it's a lie. Shanice isn't no one. She's someone I haven't stopped thinking about since the moment we met—hell, even before we met, I wondered what she was actually like. Maybe it's time I stopped hiding behind excuses and let her know.

Chapter 8

Shanice

Fifty-five times—that's how many times I've picked up my phone to text this man back, and I still don't even know what to say. How am I supposed to be friends with someone I have a pull this strong to? Being friends was my idea, but now I want to smack myself.

Even if I wanted to date, I wouldn't know what to do. My last "relationship" barely qualified because that lying, tiny dick demon found me. It was long distance, and he required so little attention it was perfect. There were so many signs. Shaking my head I pick up my phone and text Kennedy instead.

Me: Can I come over?

Bestie: I'm in post coital bliss.

Me: And…

Bestie: Bring wine and wings and you'll be allowed in

Me: I can go for wings.

Bestie: *wide smile emoji*

This girl is going to turn into a chicken if she eats any more, but I'm not tripping because I could kind of go for wings, too. Tablet and wine in tow, I travel a little farther east to get the wings from Harold's—the only location worth going to. Anybody from Chicago can tell you that.

There's a car blocking her driveway when I pull in front of her house. I curse and find a spot near the front. Now I'm going to have to use the front door—food and tote in tow. I push the door open and then bump it closed. My ankle twists on the curb when I reach into my coat pocket to press the lock on my key fob. I clutch the bag of food because that's what's really important. I brace to hit the ground, but strong arms wrap around me.

He grunts and pulls me back to my feet. *Saved by the stranger.* Turning, I open my mouth to say thank you and come face to face with the man I've been trying to figure out how to text all day.

"We've got to stop meeting like this."

"Kendrick?" He helps me up to my feet, but I'm confused. "Wha-what are you doing here?"

"My sister lives there." Pointing a little farther down the street, I stutter step when I see two girls looking at us with confused faces. "Who's that, Kenny?" The supposed sister yells, and he nods in response.

"Mind your business, Kaliyah!"

Awkwardly, I turn and give him an apologetic smile. "Sorry about that... She babysitting for you?"

"Hell nah. I love them, but those are my nieces. I only want kids that I can give back." Raising a brow he asks, "You sure *you* not following *me?*"

"Definitely not, I just wasn't expecting to see you here."

"Or at all?" he teases, his eyes gleaming with mischief.

My lips part, but no words come out. He's not wrong.

"Don't worry, I'll let it slide this time." He steps back, giving me space, but his gaze lingers, sending a shiver down my spine.

Nodding toward the door, I cross the sidewalk by walking around his large frame and putting in the code to unlock my best friend's gate.

At my back, he yells, "This means we were always supposed to meet because how could we never have run into each other before?"

I speak over my shoulder, wondering the same thing. "Kismet. See you later."

Though I'm clearly walking away, he is not trying to let me go. "So, you gonna keep pretending I didn't text you? Aye, who's house is this?"

"Not that it's your business, but it's Kennedy's, and I'm not pretending...I just didn't respond yet."

"Uh huh." He crosses his arms, clearly unconvinced.

We stare at each other for a minute longer than comfortable until he breaks the spell. "Well, I should get going. Gotta make sure to live my dreams," he winks, alluding to what I said last night. He gets into a Subaru. That is definitely not the car he had last night. I stare as the engine purrs to life. His glance meets mine one more time before he waves and pulls away.

Closing the door behind me, I lean against the wood and take a deep breath before walking into the kitchen. "Lucy, I'm home!"

Kennedy yells from the back hall. "Hey boo! I'm in the family room."

Slipping off my boots, I lug the bags down the hall since she has apparently decided not to help me. I find her feet kicked up—still in her robe—watching TV.

"So, you're not being productive at all today?" I joke. It's cold as hell outside. If I didn't have to make progress, I wouldn't.

"Girl, please. You should be doing nothing, too. The only reason you're up and at 'em is because you went dickless for the evening, and your legs don't feel like jello."

"Yeah, yeah. It's a personal choice. Here's your food, wench."

Finally moving from her spot, she grabs the styrofoam container from my hands and inhales the aroma of the perfectly fried chicken, then drizzles mild sauce all over and mumbles.

"I'm about to fuck this shit up." Smiling widely, she says, "You're the bestest!" She takes a bite of the steaming chicken and chews like a nutcracker since it's so hot. *Dumbass.*

"Remember that when I pull out this tablet."

Mouth full of chicken, she groans. "I don't understand why you don't pay somebody to do this shit."

"Because I'm half broke, Kennedy. I'm not borrowing more money from my dad. I've put so much into this already and I haven't made a dollar."

"Exactly! You've put so much money into it, but how is your online business going to succeed if your website isn't up to par?"

"Ouch..."

"My bad. Look..." Licking the tips of her fingers, she turns to face me. "I think you're fucking brilliant, and you know that. *But*, in *this* instance, I also think you need a professional's help. It'll make you stand out. You're already doing this as an online service—which is freaking genius and will allow people to save so much money since they aren't consulting direct. I just want you to get started on the right foot."

She's right, and I know it, but I haven't been honest about exactly how much I'm in the hole. The bonus from work will help, but there are so many moving parts and partnerships. I did the research for web developers, but the cheap end was four grand after my consultation.

I figure if I do it myself, it's only costing the actual price and that's thousands less, it's just going to take longer. It's why I accepted that job offer. Because at the end of the day, I still have bills to pay until this takes off and proves longevity. Since

I don't have a non-compete for this activity and I'm so far away from my job, I can keep doing it on the side.

My phone vibrates and pulls me out of my thoughts. It's Kendrick.

> Kendrick: my brother has been hounding me for your friend's phone number.

Again, I type and delete my response, unsure of what direction to go in.

"Girl, stop playing with that man and respond," Kennedy says, looking over my shoulder. Squinting, she says, "And he can let his brother know he ain't getting' my number."

"Damn nosy, I'm just not tryna lead him on. He's a self-appointed Grinch, and you know what Mom said."

"You and this Christmas rule." She shakes her head and sticks a mild sauce-drenched fry into her mouth. "You realize that isn't an indicator of a compatible partner, right? Mayor Augustus stole Martha May for decades, but she always belonged to the Grinch."

I love it when she speaks Christmas. "I know... I think..." Pausing, I reflect for a moment on why that quality is essential. She was right about NyShon, and I didn't listen.

"Look, you're stuck on this whole thing about not falling for a married man. Five-Oh skirts the line of being professional every day, just have him look Kendrick up and then fuck his brains out. I don't know where you got this idea that you gotta marry him. Hell, I didn't even give Khalil my number, and that man beat it *down*. Have some fun, baby. Yes, you're over thirty, but does that actually matter? It's not the 1920's. You don't have to find a husband before they're sent off to war. Text that man back before I do. It's not that deep, boo."

Turning up the TV to focus on her K-drama, she grabs her container and continues to stuff her face. She's right. *Fuck it.*

Me: This is a message

Kendrick: Are you a robot?

A smile spreads across my face as I read his response. Biting my lip, I contemplate what to respond.

Me: Is that offer for friends still on the table?

Kendrick: Girl, yes.

Kendrick: *sassy snapping gif*

Kendrick: *BFFL gif*

A snort sneaks out, and Kennedy looks at me with a raised brow. "Mmmhmm."

Me: You're too much

Kendrick: Only on days that end in y.

Rolling my eyes, I think back to the bar yesterday.

Me: You stole that from me.

> Kendrick: I'm 90% sure you got that from somewhere else.

> Me: Prove it!

There's a lag in his response, so I put my phone down and start to eat my finally cooled chicken. It's been sitting for a while now, so it's chewable. Opening one of the plastic sauce cups, I dip my wing instead of drenching. To me, it's more strategic, but Kennedy said it makes me mildly psychotic. *Some best friend she is!*

My phone buzzes when I'm halfway through my meal, and I honestly forgot I was texting. I nearly choke when I notice the screenshot is of an image search on Google showing the unlimited number of quotes people have made with the 'days that end in y' phrase.

> Me: You coulda let me have that one.

> Kendrick: Ah, you see that would be a girlfriend thing to do but you're my new BFFL and friends don't get a pass

> Me: I see how it is

> Kendrick: As long as you know

Kennedy is smirking at me when I finally put my phone down again.

"What's that look for?" I sit straighter on the couch instead of leaning onto the table.

"Oh, nothing. Eat your chicken so we can watch a romcom and drink that bottle of wine."

Now that sounds like a plan. Forget the website for tonight. I've got wings, wine, and maybe—just maybe—a little hope for something more with Kendrick.

Chapter 9

Kendrick

The weekend wasn't as eventful as I hoped, but I spent all Sunday texting Shanice, so I'll take it as a win. Based on her emails, I always knew she was intriguing, but she's funny as hell. My anti-holiday soul cringed when she sent me a picture of her living room packed with Christmas shit, but I can't deny it reminded me a little of Gran.

"Mornin' Bossman. You're awfully happy today." Marshall's greeting pulls me back to reality. He's sitting at his desk with his hands clasped. He's up to something.

Stopping, I narrow my gaze. "Why do you sound and look like you're about to fuck up my day?"

"It's not me, I promise."

"There's something you aren't telling me. How pissed off am I gonna be?"

"On a scale of what?"

"Marshall…"

"You know the Holiday Fever events we host for our clients every year? Well, Haverly just announced the host."

"Hell nah. Email her back and tell her I quit."

"Now Kendrick—"

"Marshall, don't you start that promotion shit, again."

"And why the hell not? If you get a promotion, I get a promotion, and I deserve a promotion!"

"How the fuck am I supposed to host events for shit I hate?"

"That's why you have me!" Grinning, he continues, "You can't seriously think the hosts plan events. We just need to get ideas to the committee and then you act as host. Easy peasy."

"Easy peasy my ass. I'll be in my office sulking."

Smiling widely, he waves. "Sounds good! Happy sadness."

I close the door behind me, much more forcefully than necessary, but it makes my point.

For the first few hours of the day, I ignore reading the dreaded email stating I get the "privilege" of hosting the holiday events for our company. Lunchtime is rolling around, and I need to know what I've been pulled into.

From: Haverly@Chi.WebDesign.com
Subject: Holiday Fever!
Holiday greetings, Everyone!
I hope you had a great weekend and are ready to turn up the holiday cheer-peture. (See what I did there?) As always, one of our lucky employees gets to host the client holiday events with the celebrations team! This year's theme is 'Classic Christmas', and our lucky representative is Kendrick Thompson!
Give it up for Kendrick, everyone :)
Best,
Haverly Lyons
Senior Executive Developer
Chi Web Design

Great, just fucking great. This is going to be a nightmare. I've never even decorated my desk with so much as an ornament, and I'm pretty sure last year I bah-humbugged a few people in the halls, but now I'm expected to host three events and the company holiday party. I'm so deep in thought I nearly missed the yellow ping in our office Collab app. That's Marshall's announcement that Haverly is on her way.

"Knock knock!" She chirps, knocking gently on the door.

"Hey Haverly, I just saw the email."

"About that…"

Is this the out I need? "If you need to choose someone else, I totally get it. Thanks for thinking of me, though."

Waving off my suggestion, she leans against my desk. "That's not it. I wanted to make sure you understood what's at stake here. No one has ever made it to senior partner without heading up a client event."

"Can't I do the summer one instead?"

"You've vetoed every event for the last five years, Kendrick. Robert takes client participation very seriously and thinks the best way to bring in more clients is to show the current ones how much we appreciate their business. You're the only person currently in this company that I believe is fit to take my position one day, but you can't do that if you don't get your head out of your ass and do what it takes to get to the next level."

"I hate this shit, Haverly. You *know* I hate Christmas. Why didn't you force me to do one of the other ones?"

She softens her tone and says, "Because I remember a time when you didn't. You've been through a lot in the last few years and yes, maybe it's easier to hate things than to face them, but I don't think you actually hate Christmas, Kendrick."

Her words hit harder than I'd like to admit. I've been here long enough that she's seen my transition, but I don't know if I'm ready to face what this all means.

Haverly snaps her fingers excitedly, then says, "I've got it. You just need someone to go with you. My niece just moved back to town and could use a good man to show her around. Why don't I ask her to come?"

"No!" Clearing my throat, I try to think of a good enough excuse. "I mean, I don't think that's a good idea. I um… I already have a girlfriend."

"You have a girlfriend?"

Shit, I guess we're both confused at what the fuck just came out of my mouth, but I have to go balls to the wall with this now.

Grasping at straws, I continue lying, "Yeah, it's getting pretty serious. We wouldn't want to start any problems, right?"

"Oh ok. She must be a great girl. I'm happy for you and Ms—." She pauses, waiting for me to fill in a name that I don't have.

I can't say she-devil's name because she knows how that went. Just then, my phone buzzes on my desk and I smirk, looking at the picture from this weekend I saved as her contact photo.

"Shanice?" She questions, looking at the name on my phone screen.

"Yeah, Shanice." My eye twitches from the lie, but it's necessary.

"That name sounds familiar."

Fuck, I didn't think about the fact that she's been heavily involved in this project with AAI. I'm such an idiot. I attempt to cover my ass and say, "Yeah, it's a pretty common name."

"Hmm, okay then. I can't wait to meet Ms... Shanice."

When she leaves my office, I collapse against the back of my chair. She's going to kick my ass for this.

I've contemplated what to say for the last few hours, but the first event is this weekend, and I need to see if I need to pay someone to go with me. Pulling out my phone, I open our text thread. If she says no, I'll just fake a breakup or something.

Me: So, I may have panicked…

Less time than I expected passes before she texts me back.

Shanice: *looking eyes emoji*

Me: My boss signed me up to be the company representative at the holiday parties we are sponsoring

Shanice: Aw, the chair of cheer

Me: Will you stop quoting the Grinch, please?

Rolling my eyes, I try not to smirk.

Me: ANYWAY. My assistant and I talked about ice skating and tree lighting then a soup kitchen volunteering and wrapping presents for kids.

Me: And we have to go to the company party too.

Shanice: …

Shanice: We who?

Me: It does seem like your type of fun, huh?

Shanice: WTF is happening right now, Kendrick?!

Tapping my fingers against the desk, I clear my throat and say, "Fuck it," aloud, even though no one is around to hear me. Four rings pass, and I nearly regret taking the risk when she answers.

"I'm hoping you're calling to explain that you're not asking me what I think you're asking me."

"*Please*, Shanice?" I'm not too proud to beg. "If you don't go, I'll have to go with my boss's niece." Lowering my voice to a whisper, I shoot my best shot. "Also, I tripped up and said that I couldn't go with her because I have a girlfriend named Shanice."

"Why the hell would you say my name? We just met for real like three days ago."

I can't believe it's only been three days. When I'm texting her, it feels like talking to someone I've known my whole life.

"That's why I said I panicked. You had just texted me, and I forgot I have your contact picture as the one of us from the bar when we met, and I was all smiling and shit. One plus one equals two, and she guessed that you were the girl. I just agreed to it because then I would look like a liar *and* a cheater...*Please*." I emphasize.

Her line goes silent, and I take the phone off my ear to make sure she's still there.

"This isn't a ploy to make me date you?"

What? "Of course not. I couldn't actually date someone who loves Christmas."

"Pfft. As if I could date someone who hates Christmas."

"So, we're in agreement. You'll go with me?"

She groans dramatically. "I can't believe you're askin' me to be your fake girlfriend. You're killin' me, smalls."

"Is everything you say a line from a movie?"

"I don't know, *Kendrick*. Isn't that something my *boyfriend* would know?"

Tou-*fuckin*-Che'.

Chapter 10

Shanice

"You told him yes tho', didn't you?" Kennedy guesses accurately. I had to call my girl when I got home. I just knew she wasn't going to believe this, but apparently, I'm predictable to her.

Flopping onto my bed, I groan and put her on speaker. "Basically. I feel like I'm doing everything you're not supposed to do when meeting someone new. He could be a serial killer."

"Bitch, with as much true crime as you've listened to, you're more likely to be one. I'm not in the room but pretend I'm holding your hand when I say this—Babe, you're doing too much right now, and you need to chill out. You put yourself on this no men rule but how the hell are you supposed to meet good men if you push them away? Just keep that pum-pum in your pants and go from there. Plus, he asked you to do him a favor, not marry him. You know you love that shit; you might as well have some fun."

Chewing my lip, I stare at the ceiling. "I guess you're right."

"Of course I am. Mama Nessa would be all over this if she was still here. She'd be helping with outfits and everything."

At the mention of Mom, my chest tightens as grief threatens to pull me under again. *I miss my mama.*

Snapping for my attention, she asks, "Outside of getting to do Christmas stuff, what are you getting out of this deal?"

"Huh?" My head tilts and my eyebrows wrinkle from confusion.

"You'll be doing a lot to help *him*. What are *you* getting out of this deal?"

I didn't know I was supposed to ask for anything. If I ask him for something, does this make this more transactional and less like real dating?

"I didn't ask for anything. I just figured this was a good way to get in some celebrating for Mom since I didn't plan much yet."

Mumbling under her breath, she says, "I'ma smack the shit out of her the next time I see her." Louder, she continues, "Didn't you say he was a web developer? Ask him to do your website. "

Damn, that's actually... a great idea! *But how do I do it after the fact?* "Isn't it too late to bring it up?"

"Shit, it's never too late to negotiate."

"You talkin' 'bout this like it's a job for real."

"It damn near is, because now y'all have to actually get to know each other so you can pretend like you're together. Now, I love you, but I gotta remind you that you fall faster than my grandma. Don't forget it's a job if you're opposed to a relationship."

Biting my lip, I contemplate what she's saying. I didn't think about us having to get to know each other. I figured I'd show up, and he would be able to do all the talking. "He hates Christmas, and you know what mama said. There might be some sexual tension, but we're friends. I'm not falling for him."

"Sure, babe, and I'm about to marry Santa Claus. Call me back. Love youuuu." After blowing kisses into the phone, she hangs up.

In the kitchen, I start dinner early. I've perfected cooking for one, but it involves a lot of prep work and vacuum sealing. Preheating the oven, I prep my potato because it's double-baked potato night. Dancing in my kitchen, I'm confused when my doorbell rings.

Looking out the peephole, I see a flower delivery.

"You can leave them on the porch, thanks!" I say through the intercom on the app.

Once I'm sure the delivery driver is gone and check the other cameras to make sure no one else is around, I open the door to grab the flowers. I'm paranoid as shit, I know, but Kennedy wasn't wrong when she said I used to listen to a lot of true crime. The cold breeze smacks me in the face as my breath turns to particles in the wind and the cold air travels beneath my oversized shirt, *whoa there now.*

Once the locks are back in place, I admire the colorful arrangement that looks more like spring than Christmas. The card is tucked underneath a pink rose.

My lips curl as I read the message written in beautiful calligraphy. 'I miss you Nicey, please call me - Nyshon.'

"Oh, hell no." Braving the Chicago cold again, I set the flowers back onto the porch. I hope he drives by to see them frozen and unwanted, just like him. This man has lost his ever-loving mind. Finger trembling, I unblock his contact and type my demands.

Me: Do not call me.

Me: Do not text me.

Me: Do not send flowers to my fucking house again, you conniving, cheating, asshole before I find and tell your wife. Don't play with me.

Bubbles show in the chat like he's typing, but I block the number again. I turn on my angry girl playlist to distract myself and continue cooking dinner. I'm not Chef Carla Hall, but I know what I'm doing sometimes. Dancing in the kitchen makes me feel closer to Mom. Every meal had to have movement with her. Even in her final days, she was full of life.

As the rotation timer on my potato goes off, another annoying bee-boop-boop-bee starts chiming from my phone. Seeing that it's Kendrick, I press decline.

"Dammit," I hiss from the burning pain from my bare finger touching the burning tray. The growing hole in the oven mitt I keep forgetting to throw away got me again. Dunking the abused oven mitt into the trash, I say, "That's what you get for being a bad-built hoe."

"Well, that's one way to answer the phone."

Squealing, I spin on my feet and find Kendrick's amused face staring up at me from the counter. I must have accidentally answered the call instead of declining. "Well, maybe that's because I didn't mean to answer the phone, *sir*."

"Ooh, I like that. Say it again."

"Fuck off," I laugh. "I burned my fingers, ergo me thinking that I clicked decline."

"Ergo, huh? That's a big word for Elmo."

Doubling over with laughter, I respond, "I hate you. Why you calling me?"

"I figured you would have some requests for me."

Caught off guard, I get quiet. *How did he know that I would ask something of him?* Maybe that was just the next natural step since he asked me something big. "And if I do?"

"Come on, woman, I don't have a lot to offer, but what do you need? I'm asking a lot, and my sister said that I should pay you, but I'm not rich out here for real."

Propping the phone against an unlit candle on the counter, I tilt my head and smile. "Since you asked, I do have two teeny things."

His brow arches as he leans back onto his couch. "What you got?"

"So, I've been trying to branch out and create my design firm that will be based online, and I've been having a difficult time because I am what they called technologically challenged."

"Ya don't say..." He laughs, "And you need me to help you finish it? You're donating your time. I can do the same."

"So, is that a yes?"

"Yes, Shanice, if you need exact words – it's a yes. Now we have the fun part."

"And what's that?"

His smile spreads, and a wave of goosebumps travels over my skin. "We gotta get to know each other, Sweets."

The tingles stop as I fake gag. "Oh God, don't call me that. It's probably one of the cringiest nicknames on the planet. Next, you're gonna say it's because you think I taste sweet. Gimme a break."

His chest rises with every bout of laughter. "That's funny as hell. I'm not about to say no lame shit like that. You 'bout as sweet as a blunt."

"Ooh, does that mean you smoke?" I know a lot of men are against women smoking. Not that I give a fuck, but it's just the facts.

Smirking, he props his phone against something and reaches under his coffee table, pulling out a fancy ass box. After inputting his code into the box, I see the lovely buds of green inside the clear container as he raises his brows.

"It's almost time for that nighttime relaxation, Ms. Ma'am."

I take my phone to my bedroom, open my own stash side drawer, and pull a pre-roll out of the plastic. "After dinner, it's about that time for me, too."

"What you cookin'? Can you cook for real, or you play cookin'?"

"What the hell is play cookin'?"

"Hear me out, I was dating this one girl, and she would sneak and buy takeout then pretend she cooked it. I swear to God, I was taking out the trash once, saw hella takeout containers, and figured it out. So again, are you cookin' cookin' or play cookin'?"

I mount my phone on the holder I use to body-double with Kennedy because I hate actually holding the phone. On the mount, I angle the camera toward the bowl as I mash, butter, and season the potato before filling a piping bag and swirling it back into the potato exterior for the second bake. To flex real quick, I finally utilize this fancy-ass shredder I bought from the Clock app to shred some gouda cheese to sprinkle on the top for that perfect crust.

"My God."

"Why your face so close to the camera?"

Lifting his shirt to show the smooth abs on his stomach, he teases, "Didn't you see that grumble? I'm jealous."

Inhaling sharply, I'm happy my face isn't on camera. Granted, this is my first time seeing under his shirt, but he seems so clean-cut. I didn't expect the tattoos etched into his skin. Snapping out of lust, I say, "I make meals for one."

"Yeah, yeah. How did you magically get this thing to hold your phone up? You an influencer, too?"

"I sell feet pics online. That's why I can afford to live by myself." I'm clearly fucking with him, but for some odd reason, he looks like that's acceptable. *Who is this man?*

"Lemme see 'em."

"How about you pay for it?"

Pulling out his tablet, he challenges, "Bet, what's the username?"

"Fool, why you taking this so seriously? It was a joke."

"I know. I just wanted to see how far you would take it."

"Yeah, sure. What gave away that it was a joke? I took acting classes in high school, so I know I ain't slip up."

"Oh, the acting skills were top-notch, but there's no way someone who was selling feet pics, which I don't shame at all, *but...* There's no way that person wouldn't immediately ask about monetary compensation for what I'm asking you to do.

I'm not calling them desperate. It's the opposite. I think they know their worth and aren't afraid to ask."

"Oh, and you think I don't know my worth?"

With his head tilted, he studies me for a second. "Not yet."

Temporarily, I'm stunned. Homie has game; I'll give him that. Clearing my throat, I use that as my escape. "I've got to go. I actually need to make this salad really quick for dinner. I'll text you later."

Resigned, his head falls. "Alright, I get it. Send me a pic when you're done. You know the presentation is just as important."

"You over there doing all that, and you haven't shown me anything but some green. I've got to go, though. *Byee*." I disconnect the call, but his words linger even after we hang up. Chopping up my vegetables, I add them to a small side plate and reflect on my perfectly individually sized portions for meals.

Is this sad? Is this really what I want to do for the rest of my life? Shaking it off, I start slicing the cucumbers. What I'm doing works for me now. There's no need to look that far into the future.

With a glass of wine, I finish the setup and place my pre-roll onto the dessert plate. Snapping a quick pic, I text it to him. It doesn't take him long to respond.

> Kendrick: Aight, aight… you know what you doing a lil bit.

My fork is halfway to my mouth, salad loaded, as another message comes through. Using my knuckle to put in the code, I laugh when I see a picture of a pizza puff inside of a styrofoam container drizzled with mild sauce. While this looks amazing—and I would smash it if it was in front of me—one thing is clear. *That man definitely isn't a cook.*

Chapter 11

Kendrick

> Me: Morning Chef *smirk emoji* First event is Friday evening at the skating rink in Millennium Park. The email said there will be food trucks too.

> Shanice: Don't start your bullshit this early in the day.

> Me: What you mean, my bullshit? We just now gettin' started.

> Shanice: And yet, I'm already your girlfriend somehow.

The growing smile on my face falls when she follows up with a correction.

> Shanice: Fake gf I mean. Anything important I should know?

> Me: I'ma make you my real friend before this is all over.

> Shanice: I meant something important like allergies.

> Me: I'm allergic to avocado

> Shanice: …

> Me: ???

Her next response is a text with a voice note laughing. *Man whatever.* Putting my phone to the side, I open my email and go to the most recent AAI response. Lanada has only requested reasonable changes since that call last week and thankfully, Shanice doesn't have to deal with any of it.

She starts a new position today, and I'm itching to ask her how it's going, but I also don't wanna be too clingy. We've chatted a bit about the design for her website. I will admit it's going to be difficult, but it's a good challenge.

How the hell did she think she was going to do this on her own?

I did say I wanted to start helping more small businesses, so it's still benefitting the path I want to take in my career, too.

"Knock, knock." Marshall is standing in the doorway with a neatly wrapped box. "From the boss lady. A gift for your lady friend, it seems."

I stand and reach to grab it from him, but he pulls it away from my grasp.

"Are you going to give me the box or…"

"Who is she? We didn't vet this woman to see if she was a psycho like your ex."

"You're right," I say, snatching the box. "We didn't vet her. I did, and she's good. Besides…" I motion for him to come closer. Once he is a breath away, I whisper, "It's not a real relationship, more of a beneficial arrangement."

He purses his lips like something stinks and asks, "Like an escort or something?"

"Man, hell nah. She's cool and happens to love Christmas. It's perfect. She'll make me look good."

"If you say so. Don't get her pregnant."

"It's not even gonna get to that point, man. You trippin'."

He studies me and then asks, "You got a picture?"

On my phone, I scroll to the one I took that night and turn it for him to see. "Here."

He mumbles, "Yeah right. That's a wife, not a fake girlfriend." Louder, he asks, "What's her name?"

This is the part when things get tricky. "It's uh… it's Shanice."

"Shanice? Why does that name—Wait, AAI Shanice? Email Shanice?!" Marshall looks like I just told him Santa was real.

"You ain't gotta yell man. Yeah, it's her."

"Oh, you're *fuuuuucked*." He leaves my office cackling. I hate that word, but it's the perfect word to describe his obnoxious laughter. Inside the box is an oversized company t-shirt. Haverly might be a very stylish woman, but this ain't it. At least I have a new shirt to wear to bed at night.

The day is long, but I survive on meager snacks until evening. My Collab app pings on my computer.

Marshall: Hoagies are here. It's five.

He's the best assistant I've ever had. Not that 'assistant' accurately describes his position, but they would only allow me to give him a raise until he graduates. He's smart as shit and is working on his coding degree. I'm not going to judge the fact that he decided to go to college later in life. I couldn't imagine being a marine.

Today is our mentorship night, so I hang back even though I'm tired. Truthfully, I think I can use his help with Shanice's website.

The mouthwatering scent of sautéed peppers, onions, and buttered rolls from the hot sandwiches fills the office as he enters. After we eat, I role-play as the annoying client while he practices deciphering what they actually need.

"What do you think about a multi-select drop with horizontal branching?" This one will be a challenge because I'm speaking like someone who doesn't know code. Clients "research" in an effort to be helpful, but all it does is make things confusing.

"Horizontal? Like externally? Would there be multiple drop downs under a single item, so each drop down points the customer to a unique external link?"

"Great job, there."

"Thank the Lord, I almost missed what you were saying with that one. What's this for?"

"Shanice has this really interesting idea on how to combine interfaces. She wants to have a website where her paid members can go through and pick their own designs based on algorithm profiles instead of paying a huge consultation fee. For her, it's a lot more about cataloging and updating the algorithms than having to meet with individual clients all the time. It's pretty revolutionary for those who don't like people for real."

Marshall's smile builds the more I've talked.

"What?"

"Oh nothing... You know a lot about her goals for this to be someone you're not interested in. It's curious, right?"

"Get the fuck on, man. I had to ask her about the details because I'm doing that in exchange for her coming to the events. It's going to save her thousands and the least I could do."

"Sure, it is." Marshall cuts his eyes away and then asks, "You want my help?"

"Yeah, I think we can add it to your portfolio."

"Alright, let's do it then."

Three hours. That's how long we spent working through all the details and planning her website. If this works, it will probably be the most unique interface we've ever built, and I'm excited for the challenge.

Finally, home, I kick off my shoes at the door and toss my keys onto the counter. The room is quiet, save for the soft hum of the fridge. My stomach grumbles, but the thought of eating leftovers again doesn't excite me. Instead, my mind drifts to Shanice.

I glance at my phone. Her last message—a voice note laughing at my avocado allergy—replays in my head, and a slight grin spreads across my face. My thumb hovers over the call button. What would I even say? *Hey, just wanted to hear you laugh at me some more.*

I shake my head, tossing the phone onto the couch. "Get it together, man." Then again, do I need a reason to call my friend?

Chapter 12

Shanice

Restless, I pace around my kitchen, trying to convince myself I don't want to talk to him. I've also been hoping that he does call, and that's a fucking problem because we're just friends—*and I hate it.*

Friends can look forward to talking to other friends, right? I find myself picking up my phone because I want to hear his voice. That's fucking crazy, right? Strong connections like this can't happen in real life. I'm not saying I'm in love with him because that's psychotic, but I feel like he could be...like we could be something.

The timer beeps on the slow cooker for dinner. I grab a bowl and get the grease started for the final touch. After rewashing my hands, I cut strips of corn tortillas. There's nothing like homemade chips. It doesn't take long to fry them, and the hollow crunch of fresh chips makes these extra few minutes worth it.

Behind me, my phone rings on the counter, interrupting my thought process and startling me back into the now. It buzzes across the surface, and I nearly miss the call, trying to make sure I don't burn the tortillas. Seeing his name on the screen has my heart beating triple time. Before it goes to voicemail, I swipe to answer and wait for him to talk to make sure I didn't just make this up in my head. The line is silent, but he's probably waiting for me to speak.

"Shanice... you there?"

Sucking my lips in, I silently scream and bounce on my toes like a teenager when the cute boy in school calls her.

"I'm—" My throat constricts a little, so I clear it before talking again. "I'm here, I just got done with dinner."

"Ah ok. I was tryna see what you were on. I was thinking about you, and I know you were thinking about me, so I thought maybe we should think about each other–together. Hopefully, with some dinner because I'm starving."

He's thinking about me.

I'm thinking about him.

Let's go to dinner.

Together.

He just asked me on a date... "Oh. That's kind of you, but I just cooked, and, *emotional damage*, I don't like to waste food."

"Oh, alright then. What'd you cook?"

"I made some chicken tortilla soup. What you in the mood for? I can give a suggestion."

"Right now, I think I could go for some soup."

My eyes roll around my head as I think quietly to myself. We probably should hang out, so we aren't awkward around each other. "You remember how to get to Morgan Park?"

There's a shuffling sound, then he sounds a little farther away. "I can make it out south tonight." The sound of a faucet overpowers his voice, so I barely hear what he's saying until the water turns off and I catch the end, "—the sports center?"

"Yeah, I'm close to the sports center."

Keys jingle, a door closes, and the startup of an ignition sounds in rapid succession. "It wouldn't be a problem for me at all, actually. I haven't had a home-cooked meal in a long time, and maybe we can get a few more questions to make this believable. I got an email about the second event next Sunday if you're free, but we can look at that together. Can you send me your address?"

"Oh yeah, right." I opened our text thread and added my address to the mix.

"Got it. Remind me to show you how to share a ping for your location. Alright, I'll focus on driving, and then I'll be there soon. GPS says twenty-five minutes but I'm going for twenty-two."

"It's not a race speedy."

"It is if it means I get to spend more time with you."

He's such a smooth talker. "Oh okay. Right, see you in a bit." I slam my phone onto the counter hard enough to crack the screen. I should be panicking with how expensive this thing was, but that's why I bought this durable case. but I'm panicking. I just invited this man to my home. This isn't that crazy, right? I've done crazier things with people I didn't know at all. *Fuck it.* I think about how much I can get done in twenty minutes. That's plenty of time. At least, I hope it is.

There isn't much to clean around the house, but I quickly straighten up the front room and vacuum the carpet. The last ten minutes are spent washing off the day. I usually take a shower after dinner because it helps to calm me, but I'm not trying to have any doubt that I don't stink. My outfit is more about comfort than cute, but I'm not trying to do too much. While lotioning my ankles, the doorbell chimes. *He's here.*

Each step to the door makes me nervous, because the last man I let enter my space tore my heart to shreds. Before I open the door, I inhale and exhale focused breaths to move past the apprehension then plaster on a smile.

"Hey," he says, sounding just as nervous as I am.

"Welcome to my little house." I open the door wide for him to enter.

Like his mama raised him well, he takes his shoes off at the door and hangs his coat before looking around. His shock is visible as he asks, "Uh, did you know you have a vase of frozen roses sitting on your porch?"

Ah hell. I forgot about those damn flowers. When I saw them this morning, they were wilted and cold. I'll take them to the trash later. Well, maybe I'll keep the vase. Those always come in handy. "My ex doesn't want to accept leave me alone as an answer, apparently."

"That's not cool."

"No, it isn't. Especially since he neglected to tell me that he—Never mind." I can't believe that I just almost admitted out loud that I was sleeping with a married man. It wasn't knowingly, but does that really make it any better? Instead of voicing my thoughts, I say, "The food is ready. Lucky for you, soup is the only thing I don't make in single portions."

"Lucky for me, indeed." His eyes flit around, and his expression changes from various levels of shock to terror as he takes in the decor covering nearly every square foot. I haven't quite figured out where everything should go. His nose curls as he notices the fireplace, and I'm mortified. That's where all of Grandma's phallic-shaped ornaments are lying. *Why didn't I think to put those away?*

"Are those dicks?" He steps backward and asks, "Why do you have dick-shaped ornaments?"

"They're not mine, and they're not real." His eyebrow lifts and I think I'm on borrowed time. "They're my mom's. Actually, they were Grandma's. Mom put them up every year, and I didn't know what to do, so I just put them there in the meantime. I promise that's not a normal ornament for me."

"You *really* love this holiday."

"I do. My mom passed last year. Now, I'm celebrating for her. I'll maybe skip the peenaments next year."

He laughs when I say peenaments, then gets a little more serious. "I'm sorry to hear about your mom. Is your uh... is your kitchen as... festive?"

"Come on, I normally eat while watching TV, but I think you'll like it here more." The kitchen doesn't have much besides some wreathing across the top of the cabinets, some nutcrackers, a Santa's village on the buffet, and a Grinch cookie jar.

"Hey, look it's you." I joke.

He spots the cookie jar and chuckles. "How can I help?"

"I've got it. It's only soup."

"Yeah, but I left in such a rush I didn't bring anything. I have to be useful somehow."

"For real, everything is done. Just have a seat."

He listens, watching intently as I move about the kitchen to grab bowls, silverware, and cups. It takes me no time, but once the table is set, I feel awkward. It's the weirdest non-date I've ever had.

He places his hands palm up on the table. *Oh, he prays.*

"Is this okay? I can pray by myself if you're not comfortable with it."

"No, no this is good. It's just... new."

The prayer is quick, and he doesn't fumble over his words, but it makes me wonder more about him.

"You a church boy?" I ask.

The corner of his lip tilts. "Nah, I mean... *maybe* when I was younger, but I haven't been inside a church in a while. I'm more spiritual than anything else. Church isn't restricted to four walls. The Bible says the church is the body of Christ, and since we were made in His image, we are the church. It's two of us here, so God is here."

"Oh, you know your beliefs for real."

"I try, but I also believe that everyone has their own rights to their thoughts and beliefs. That's why I asked first."

"Before my mama died, I was stronger in my faith." To distract myself from the pain, I stir my spoon around the bowl. A tear falls against my will, splashing into the soup.

I didn't realize he was still watching until he says, "My gran would have loved your house. She was my rock. My parents were great, but Gran got me. I spent summers with her and any break I was allowed to. At first, I thought she was lonely.

Grandad passed a couple years after I was born, and she never remarried. As I got older, I realized she just loved me. She was my go-to person when she was taken from the world—Let's just say I haven't been the same. It's been almost three years since we lost her. I don't understand your exact pain, but I can empathize with losing someone close to you."

"Thank you." I hate when people say I understand—unless they've lost someone and know what it feels like.

"No problem, grief is a journey—a cycle. Just know that I'm always here for you, no judgments." He uses the tongs to scoop some of the homemade chips on top of his soup and then takes a bite. His eyes widen more with every chew until they roll. Once he swallows, he pushes back from the table and gets down on one knee in front of me.

I laugh and push him away. "You play too much. It's not that good."

"Are you insane? This shit fye. Obviously, I just wanted to see you, but I think I gotta move in now. This how you cook every day?"

"Not every day, but yeah, I try. Mama taught me how to cook. She used to say a good meal is the key to a man's heart, but I didn't expect you to fall to a knee after one bite." I take a bite of my soup and enjoy the warmth as it spreads across my body. Soup for dinner is fantastic and one of my favorite things to cook in the winter. It's also easy to toss into the slow cooker so I can come home to a warm meal.

I know I enjoy my food without words, but it's too quiet. Opening my eyes, I catch the bob of his throat as he sucks his bottom lip.

"I need to eat at the kitchen counter or something."

Shaking it off, he keeps eating without looking at me. I didn't do anything offensive, I hope. *Why is he avoiding looking at me?* I twist the back of my spoon to check my reflection and ensure nothing is wrong. Sure enough, I look like me. Just a *confused* me.

His phone vibrates on the table. Out of instinct, I look up and see the name Mark on his screen. His brows pinch at the message, but he slides it into his pocket and then finally looks at me again.

"Would you hate me if I got another bowl?"

Some of the tension I've been holding eases away. *I need to get the fuck out of my head.* "Nah, it's okay. It will save me from eating it four days this week."

"How about I take you to dinner before we go ice skating? I owe you now, and there is a restaurant close by."

"I thought there were food trucks at the venue."

"There are, but I can't imagine eating from one for real. I'm squeamish."

"Like blood squeamish or germs only?"

"I plead the fifth."

"Come on, isn't this something a girlfriend should know?" I bump my foot against his and laugh.

"We're new, that's explainable enough."

He knocks on the table nervously, then asks, "Dinner?"

Chewing on my bottom lip, I say, "Raincheck, maybe? I already had to ask to leave early for these events, and I just started this job."

"Or you can come with me anyway and say fuck 'em."

"Kendrick Lamar Thompson!" I don't know if that's his middle name but it's funny as hell to me.

His laugh is deeper and louder than I've heard so far. "So, funny story, my name was supposed to be Kendrick Lamar, but at some point, Dad took our bracelets off in the hospital. We didn't have those fancy alarms like kids have now. My mom had a fucking fit, and they switched our middle names. Instead of Kendrick Lamar, I'm Kendrick Lavan, and my twin is Khalil Lamar. Life worked out the way it was supposed to. My sister is Kaliyah Leah, which means absolutely no damn sense to me. It was the worst possible name they ever could have thought up, apparently."

"Wait. Did you say Kaliyah Leah?"

"Unfortunately."

"Poor girl. It's pretty, but it rolls off the tongue just a little too much."

"She knows for sure. No shade to my brother because I love him, but Kaliyah is my girl. That's my best friend, and those babies are basically my kids. Not that we're on a dating interview, but if anyone asks about kids at one of the events, it would be a definite no from me."

Gulping down a glass of water, I take a second to respond. "It would be a no from me too, but that isn't up for discussion." I probably didn't need to add that second part because it will only cause more questions than I want to answer.

He eyes me quietly and then stands to refill his bowl. Thankfully, he doesn't press for more information. I continue eating, but my appetite is withdrawing. I don't know what to say next. People always say I'll change my mind, but this isn't something I can do anything about, and I'm not in the mood to have that conversation right now.

Losing a pregnancy will teach you that it's not always about what you did or didn't do. Sometimes, it just is what it is. Let's be real. Getting away from that man was probably a saving grace, but that didn't make the hurt lessen.

My ovaries and uterus are gone now—cancer took those. I had a choice to make. It was either me or the baby. Maybe I lived long enough for treatment, maybe I didn't, and we both died. But if my baby lived and I died, they would've had to live with a man who thought dragging me across the floor was a light punishment. With that in mind, my choice was clear. My battle with cancer ended, and so did my possibility of bearing children.

Intrusive thoughts are spiraling in my brain, but I need to run away from this thought process. I ask, "What do you do around the holidays since you don't like them?"

"Things I do at other times of the year—live my life. My bills still need to be paid. I still gotta eat." He lifts his spoon with more soup, then continues, "It's honestly harder to *avoid* all of this bullshit. Everyone wants me to donate, but I donate all year long. Doing it only around the holidays is performative. The older I got, the more I realized Christmas is a cash grab. The prices get higher, they advertise toys on TV *all fuckin' day long*." He breaks some tortillas in his hands, sprinkles the crunchy bits on top of his soup, and then shrugs. "I still buy gifts for my nieces, but I buy them shit all year. It's just a day, but people go into debt up to their chins to prove something folks should already know. What's the reward? That is my question."

I'm flabbergasted. I've never heard someone go so far down a rabbit hole about Christmas like this before. *He really hates it.*

"Are you asking what the reward of *giving* is?"

"Yeah, what's the reward?" He leans his elbows on the table, and it makes me itch.

"I didn't know you had to get a reward for being a good person. Why do you have to gain anything? Can't it just be about being nice?"

"Yeah, there's that whole 'Santa Claus' mentality. You're "good" around holidays, so you can convince people to add you to their list, but then the rest of the year you're barely providing support."

"Okay, so what about the kids who don't have this yearly support you speak of? Is it right for them to wake up to nothing when these advertisements are blasted in front of them on TV all day? You have other kids at school who are coming back wearing new gym shoes and clothes, bragging about electronics and games. What about the elderly who are alone? What about making sure people feel loved during a time when depression spikes and all they have are reminders of things they've lost and the position they're in? *That's my reward.* Seeing even one smile brighten is all I need."

"And I love that for you. All I'm saying is keep that energy all year round. How you think those people feel when folks don't show up afterward? Is their depression mysteriously gone? One day of joy doesn't cancel out the pain they feel during the rest of the year. Getting new toys doesn't change little Timmy's leg from being broken, nor the pain in his belly when he wakes up a couple of days later, and the only thing in the cabinets is cereal."

Ouch. I don't think he meant to make me feel bad, but now I feel like shit. I've never thought about it that way. In my mind, it's a way to spread the love I feel. Leaving the statement where it is, I stand and clear the table. My mind is racing, and apparently, he can tell. Quietly, he gets up to help me load the dishwasher. Weirdly enough, we're in sync, as if we've done this a million times before, but this is our first time hanging out since meeting in person. All of our interactions have been through emails, texts, and calls. Granted, we text a lot, but that's how new friendships are, *right?*

He turns me to face him, then lifts my wobbling chin as tears threaten to spill. "What's going on inside of that little peanut head of yours? I didn't mean to make you cry. I was just answering your question, Shanice."

"I know..." I wipe my eyes with the sleeves of my shirt and sniff. "I never thought about what happens after Christmas." My head falls to his chest, and he massages the back of my neck, sliding his fingers into my curls. Stepping closer, he places a wide palm across my back, and for a second, I stop breathing. Unintentionally, I bite my bottom lip. His gaze tracks the movement as lust clouds his eyes. My heart feels like it's pounding a mile a minute. He leans to rub his nose against mine. If I lean up on my tippy toes, I could just...

"*Saaaanta Claus is coming to town!*" *Fuck.* I forgot about that stupid fucking alarm clock. The spell of the moment is broken as he steps back to search for what interrupted us. I walk over to the countertop, muttering curses, and unplug the clock. If that wasn't Grandma Mae's, I would have thrown it into the garbage.

He forces out a breath, then clears his throat. "I should probably head home. I gotta be at work early in the morning. This definitely beats reheated fast-food leftovers." He fails to hide the cringe as we walk back into the living room. At the door, he turns to wrap me in a warm hug. "Thanks for inviting me over. Text me if you think of anything."

"I'll see if there's a sweater or something we can get quick so we can be all matchy like a real couple."

"Whatever you want, Babygirl. You're doing me a favor with this." He places a kiss on the corner of my mouth, and I hold my breath, wishing there was more. The hairs on my neck rise when he slides his hand through my curls and leans close to whisper, "I wish the clock didn't interrupt us, beautiful. I could've gone for dessert."

Sweet baby Jesus. I close the door behind his retreating frame and then lean against it. That man is going to ruin me, and hopefully my vagina too. In the meantime, I walk back toward my bedroom, hoping Winston is charged. He's in for a night.

Chapter 13

Kendrick

Checking my watch for the thirtieth time, I wish she would've let me pick her up. Pulling out my phone, I send a desperate text.

Me: See you soon?

I know we're coming from work to get here, but I'm anxious, and my palms are sweaty. I'm more nervous now than I was on my first date. I don't see the woman with beautiful curls and eyes that are so fucking soft and gentle I couldn't turn away once I got to see them. Man, I never had a voice kink before, but when she started talking on the other side of that nutcracker, it lured me in like a siren song.

As soon as I see the black sweater and knitted hat, we were able to get delivered, I'll feel better. Apparently, matching clothes is something people do in relationships when they go places.

"Hey, Kendrick."

I'm surprised to see my frat brother approaching. "Yo, what's good, Mark? How you doing, sands?" He went to a different university, but we crossed at the same time. I ain't seen him in years, but we keep up. I invited him to ice skating since he said he would be in town, but he said his wife wasn't going for that. I didn't expect to see him tonight.

"I'm straight bro. I just saw you walking down the street and wanted to pop over. My ole lady in the car, though, so I gotta head back before she kicks my ass."

He daps me up and then takes off at a jog toward the car beeping on the curb. Damn, he wasn't lying. She looks like she's about to curse him out.

"Kendrick..." Haverly brings my attention back to the event. "Would you like to make a toast to our clients? We should get started."

Shanice is nowhere in sight. It was already a shot in the dark, and she hasn't responded to me all day, but I'm hoping she's just fashionably late. The walk to the tiny table at the front with a microphone is quick. I'm doing my best not to bump into any of the many bell-adorned sweaters as I twist through the crowd. *Lord, when they start ice skating, they're really going to be jingling.*

After a small sip of water, I turn on the mic. "Good evening, everyone. We appreciate you all coming out tonight to celebrate. We're honored you would spend some time with us and away from your families during this season." I stretch the collar of my sweater, and then my voice cracks. "W-we hope you enjoy your evening so far. Ice skating will start in fifteen minutes. The food trucks are open with the tickets you received at sign-in."

There is a smattering of clapping pitters in the area until Haverly takes the microphone. "Alright now! Is everyone ready to get the Christmas holiday season started off right?" She says emphatically.

With a whisper, like she's telling a secret, Haverly says, "Your website was our favorite website to launch, but don't tell anyone else." Laughter builds as the guests understand her joke. I ain't think it was all that funny, but whatever.

At the back, the sea of attendees part–or maybe it's just my mind forgetting that anyone else exists as she enters. Her hips sway side to side like the sidewalk is her own catwalk. Her presence is just that radiant. Curls spill from under a knit hat. Based on her smile, she's enjoying the setup. I wish I could see the world through her eyes. Her leather pants are smooth against her like a second skin, and the way she paired a matching leather trench coat on top of her black sweater is sexy as hell. I want to see her in nothing but the trench.

"*Damn.*" I accidentally whisper into the mic. A few laughs follow, but Haverly hisses. I hand it back to her and walk off the stage.

I hear her mumble, "Young love," or some bullshit, but that's not what this is. It's admiration, but I'm happy the appearance works so far.

Shanice stops in her tracks and looks around, finally searching for me instead of observing. The crowd steps to the side, turning to see what, or who has my gaze fixed. Like a moth to a flame, she finally sees me. Shanice's steps are leisurely and uncertain compared to how I'm plowing through the crowd.

Finally, face to face, I kiss her gloved hand.

"Hey," She's being shy, and it's so cute. Maybe it's the reality of the date hitting her because she's usually more talkative. It's one of the things I like about her.

"Hey, pretty lady."

From behind, someone calls out, "After that fanfare, I need to see a kiss or something." Cheers and applause follow their statement.

Leaning close, I tuck a loose curl behind her ear. "I think we forgot people might ask us to kiss."

She wraps her arms around me for a hug, then tucks her face into my neck and whispers, "Are we really about to kiss for this first time in front of all these people?"

I look into her eyes, sparkling with life, and ask, "Do you trust me?"

My mouth is so close to hers I could stick my tongue out and lick her lips, and I'm so fucking tempted to do it. The thought turns into need, and even if I didn't plan it, I desire this—real or not. Her eyelids are low like she's been drinking, but the only thing I think she's drunk on is lust. As soon as she nods, I close the distance by sliding one hand to her lower back. The other thumb traces her lower lip. I follow with a gentle kiss, but two more follow as I quickly get addicted to the feeling of her plump and soft lips. Need takes over, and I forget we're surrounded by a crowd. I suck her lower lip into my mouth, tangling my tongue with hers. I turn my head to kiss her deeper.

She moans into my mouth and kisses me back with as much intensity as she's getting from me as she grabs the lapels of my coat. The heat of her body so close to mine makes my heart thunder in my chest. My hearing clears, and the crowd's hoots, whistles, and cheers get louder. I place three more quick kisses on her lips and her jaw, then lean her head back to kiss her collarbone. I squeeze her one more time before pulling away.

Unsteadily, she sways and mumbles, "Oh, we're in trouble."

After a kiss like that, I think she's in trouble because that feeling right there... *it's exactly where I want to be.*

From the stage, Haverly says, "Alright, show's over. Let's have as much fun as the young'uns".

I tuck Shanice's hand in mine, and we walk over to the skate rental booth. "Have you ever ice-skated before?" Switching the subject is more manageable than discussing whatever that was back there.

"Don't laugh, but I wanted to be Kristi Yamaguchi after watching figure skating, so I may or may not have taken lessons for a few years. What about you?"

"I told you I can roller skate, right?"

"Yeah, but that's not the same as ice skating. Can you inline skate, like rollerblade?"

"Uh, yeah. I'm better with four wheels, but I can rollerblade too. Is that good?"

"I think we'll find out," she mumbles next to me, then asks the attendant for a pair of skates, "May I have a size eight, please?"

"I'm surprised you didn't bring your own."

"I was tempted but took the train today and didn't feel like carrying those."

"Wait, you didn't drive? How are you getting home? The train only runs like once an hour right now."

"I know. I'm gonna rideshare home. It won't be that bad. I hate driving downtown. Y'all crazy impatient."

She's right about that. I only give about half a millisecond for the light to turn green before that first horn is honked. "You want me to take you home? It's not a big deal."

"Nah, it's okay. We both have to work in the morning, and this new position stresses me a little."

"Shanice, I can take you home. I'm the reason you're here."

"It's nothing against you. I just need to go home—alone."

I don't push, but it shouldn't be on her dime. "Will you at least let me pay for it?"

"Okay, Money Bags. Let's go skate."

We change into our ice skates and then head onto the ice. My legs wobble like newborn calves for the first minute or so, but soon enough, I've got the hang of it. Well, I have it enough to be confident I'm not going to fall on my ass and embarrass myself out here.

She's gliding around like a ballerina on the ice. Her legs cross gracefully as she leans into the turns.

With a quick maneuver—I know I can't replicate—she shifts to skate backward and says, "Distract me. Tell me about work."

I raise my arm, encouraging her into another graceful turn, and say, "There's nothing much for me to tell outside of a few annoying meetings I had to attend with Marshall to finalize pulling this shit together. What happened with your old boss?"

"Lanada's been on a rampage, and now I understand why Ted insisted I stay on his floor. Apparently, she's one more foul sentence away from being fired. I'm just excited that I can get my projects now. How's the AAI website going?"

"Oh, I finished already. Once Haverly let her ass have it, I pulled those designs together the same day, and it was wrapped up on Wednesday. Freedom never felt so good. I'm on to newer projects now. I have one I'm partnering up with my genius mentee to build. It's complicated but completely revolutionary because it gives the customer more control and direct access to vendors."

"Oh shit, that sounds cool."

"It is. I'm impressed by the idea." Laughing to myself at the apparent hint to her site. I shake my head and guide us toward the hot chocolate bar.

"Hot chocolate doesn't freak out your germ scale?"

Germ scale. *I like it.* "Nah, they're using pouches of chocolate mixed with water, and there's a scoop in the marshmallows."

She tilts her head slightly to peer at me before sitting on one of the many logs around the fire, still wearing our ice skates. "If you say so. Isn't hot chocolate a Christmas-y drink Mr. Scrooge?"

"Hot chocolate is a drink for the cold, not the holidays. Besides, even Scrooge had a reason." I thought about leaving it there for a second, but I chose to toss her carrots the same way she did for me. "My grandma was a Christmas lover. She probably would have laughed at your dick-shaped ornaments. She was special, and without her..." *What's the point?* "There's some shit revolving around my ex too, but she can burn in hell with gasoline draws on."

She laughs and says, "Make sure you save some gasoline for my ex, too." With an understanding smile, she says, "Sorry about your loss. Your grandma sounds like someone my mom would have loved. Maybe they're up there arguing with angels about how many decorations are too many. I think tonight was a success. You didn't even have to mingle with other people."

"Yeah, I'm thinking since the event was outside, it allowed me to run away from people more easily." I meet her gaze when I look up from my hot chocolate. "Meeting you here was worth it."

Her cheeks redden against her brown skin, and I smirk.

"Alright, let me see some of those Yamaguchi skills. Don't think I forgot."

"I don't know… there's a decent number of folks here. I'm not tryna end up on nobody internet."

"Come on, Beautiful. Just show me an eight-count or something short. Pleeeease."

'Every Year, Every Christmas' plays, and she skates away. I try to pay attention because I asked her to show me something, but my chest aches as I'm reminded of Grandma. She loved her some Luther. This was her favorite Christmas song. My emotions distract me, and I stutter in my glide. Shanice manages to pull up behind me, then wraps her arms around my waist to stop me from falling and certain embarrassment. I just knew we would both end up on the ground.

"Thanks, Princess. Now, I definitely have to see more."

"Don't laugh?" It comes out more like a question than a demand.

"Is that a question?"

"See, now you're making me nervous. I need a break first." She skates to the side, and I follow. We exit the rink, and she sits on a bench, dangling her feet back and forth.

I nudge her with my shoulder. "Aw, come now, Sweets. What I tell you about being nervous around me?"

She scrunches up her face, "Nothing, cuz this—."

"Ah, this is Shanice, I take it." We're removed from our momentary bubble when Haverly walks up next to us.

I sling my arm around her shoulder to look more like a couple, and she leans into me. "Shanice, this is my boss, Haverly—Haverly, Shanice."

"Lovely to meet you, dear. The last one was a real—"

"We don't have to go there," I cut in, "have you seen Robert?"

Shanice looks at me weirdly, but I haven't had a conversation with her about Rose. What would I even say? I got dumped during a proposal on Christmas Eve.

I think the fuck not.

Like we spoke to him up, Robert's gruff voice sounds behind me. "How'd you manage to wrangle this one into Holiday Fest duties?"

Shanice flinches under my arm. He talks loud as fuck for no reason all the time.

Haverly apologizes for him. "You'll have to excuse him. He doesn't know how to turn his voice volume to an appropriate level."

With a hearty laugh, he slaps a rough hand on my shoulder, pushing me forward. "Keep up the good work, young man."

"Oh, you know these events are a battle of the assistants, but Marshall is winning so far in my eyes."

"Ah, yes. That's certainly true. We have to make sure he tags along at the next event. Thanks for all you do, Kendrick. Your hard work hasn't gone unnoticed in the last year. You've really been pushing it to a senior executive-level quality. It's nice to see you mixing with our clients. They love to see their vendors in person."

I'm at a loss for words. I didn't realize he knew who I was like that. Yeah, I've been busting my ass, but to know it's noticed is... it makes it worth it.

"Who is this delightful specimen next to you?"

I cringe when he says specimen. "This is my lady, Shanice. Shanice, this is the big boss, Robert."

He waves a hand, dismissing my statement, and says, "Big boss, my ass. I just sign the checks."

"I'd say the check signer is the most important of all," Shanice jokes. She's quick with it, and once again, I'm asking myself where this woman came from. She eases into conversation with them effortlessly, and even if I don't want to compare her to Rose—it's hard not to. Rose and I were together for years, and she never attempted to converse in professional settings, let alone had the aptitude for it.

"Oh, I like this one." Haverly's smile is warm and motherly. *That's new.*

"I'm pretty fond of her myself," I say.

Shanice sips her hot chocolate when Robert elbows Haverly and says, "I see wedding bells in their future."

Shanice chokes and I pat her back like one of the girls when they were babies. She aims a questioning stare my way, but I was just trying to help.

"You alright?" I ask.

With an annoyed face, she responds, "Peachy."

Haverly and Robert leave us to talk, but she's quiet. "What's wrong?" I ask.

"Exactly how far along did you tell them we were in our relationship?"

I pull her closer, then lean down to whisper into her hair, "I didn't tell them we were engaged if that's what you're asking, and no, I'm not going to put that kind of pressure on you at any point."

Her relief is clear when our eyes meet.

Note to self—no matter how much underlying attraction there is, she definitely doesn't see you that way. *Don't get caught up with someone else who doesn't value you for more than your pocketbook.*

Chapter 14

Shanice

> Kendrick: Hey, I hope you had a good weekend.

> Kendrick: Thanks again for coming, I'll fill you in on the details for Wednesday.

> Kendrick: I'll have a website update for you soon too.

> Me: Thanks

My message is short, but I don't know what to say to him. I thought about texting him earlier, but then the day got busy. Hell, the sun already set, so clearly, he wasn't thinking about me either.

"Knock. Knock." Ted knocks on the wall of my temporary office.

"Hey, is everything okay?" Sitting up in my chair, I flip my phone on its face.

He leaves the door open but takes a seat in the lone chair. "Nothing's wrong. I'm just glad I caught you before I went home. I was thinking you could come with me to tour the Richards' property. Based on what they're looking for, I think you'd be the perfect one to get it done."

"Sir—"

"Ted," He corrects, but I feel odd calling him that.

"Ted, not to doubt your choice, but wouldn't this be better for someone more skilled?"

His brows nearly touch as he wrinkles them while pursing his lips. "Why do you think I hired you?"

Unintentionally, I shrug my shoulders and cut my eyes to the ceiling. It's unprofessional as hell, but it's better than saying 'hell if I know.' *Maybe.*

"You don't know." His tone is full of disbelief.

Softly, I admit, "I'm not great with the clients."

"That's not true at all. Every time you have a problem, who are those clients?"

"I don't know. I'm not really paying attention to who they are. I'm just trying to focus on their perception of me and how I can change it."

"Listen here, young lady. How people *perceive* you isn't your problem. Especially when I know for a fact those women have complained because you intimidate them. You wouldn't have gotten this job if you were rude or incompetent. Back to my original question, they've asked us to meet on Wednesday. Does that work for you?"

I don't know how I could possibly intimidate anyone, but whatever. Wednesday—I feel like I have something. Flipping my phone over, I see a text reaction from Kendrick and remember why Wednesday sounds familiar.

I must have my thinking face on because he asks, "Are you busy that day?"

"No...well yes, but it's after work. I need to make sure that I'm free at five."

Smiling, he asks, "Anything fun, at least?"

My smile is so wide you can probably see my molars in the back. I nod and say, "Yeah, it's definitely something fun."

"Well, whoever he or she is... I hope they keep that smile on your face." He stands. "Alright then. I'm going to head out before my wife gets upset. You really should get out of here, too. It's late."

Oh shit, it's six o'clock already. How did I manage to stay here so late? It's probably because it gets dark so early now the streetlights coming on aren't a good indication of time anymore. My phone rings again as I'm packing up my laptop to leave. I check it real quick because I'm not the text and drive person. You'll have to wait until I get to where I'm going. My car is more about purpose and function, so it doesn't read my texts aloud.

> Unknown: There's no reason for you to ignore me, Nicey

> Unknown: You know don't nobody want you the way I want you.

> Me: I mean with this with every bit of disrespect possible, fuck you.

> Me: If this is the only kind of attention, I can get I would rather be alone.

> Unknown: I love you, Nicey. You can be mad at me all you want, but you're mine.

> Me: Hmm, my pussy thinks otherwise. She has moved on.

Rolling my eyes, I block this number, too, as the text bubbles appear on the screen. That last message is going to piss him off, but I don't care. One day, this will be true, so he should accept it now. On the elevator, I'm so ready to get home. Before, I didn't realize how late it was, but now that the time has set in, the exhaustion from a long day is kicking my ass. The elevator stops, and the doors open to—Lanada. Of fucking course, I would run into her.

"Lanada," I acknowledge her presence, but she turns her nose to me and takes a step back so the elevator doors close without her. Apparently, she would rather wait than share one with me. This is a small building though, and there's only one on this side. She should have known better than to piss me off because as I'm walking out of the elevator, I press all of the lower levels, so it takes an extra few minutes to get back up to her. Out loud, I fake an "Oops!" but in my head, it's "That's what you get bitch."

An unknown call rings over and over and over again. I don't have time for this shit. Dialing 311, I call C-Mobile to get my number changed. It's a hassle, but I'm tired of ducking and dodging phone calls. He doesn't get the hint. Before I leave the job, I sit in my car and make sure everything is squared away. I've been here long enough to see Lanada come huffing and grumbling out of the office. *Karma always gets her repayment.* Five minutes later, my new number is set, and I send a text to the family chat. I'll change it at work tomorrow.

> Me: Hey, I had to change my phone number.

> 12: It would be great to know who "I" is.

> Me: *eyeroll emoji*

> Bestie: Hey boo! it's OBVIOUSLY Shanice, she's texting the group chat…stupid

> Dad: Thank you, Kennedy, I didn't realize who it was either.

Me: I need y'all to be so for real. You knew it was me.

12: Why did you have to change your number?

I should have known that he would be the one to ask that question, *dammit.*

Me: The spam calls are getting wild.

Bestie: Spam calls *crying emoji*

12: You're a horrible liar.

Dad: What's she lying about? I get those spam calls too.

Dad: Does changing your number help?

Me: Don't change your number, Dad. It's my ex. He won't leave me alone.

12: I can help with that

Bestie: *gun cocking gif* me too

12: I saw your last gun range sheet, you can't help nobody

Bestie: Well, sorry it's not my job to shoot at people all day.

Me: ooooookay, this is going left. My ex won't leave me alone and I'm tired of blocking, so I changed my number.

Me: It's not that big of a deal

Dad: I'm coming over

Me: Okeedoke. About to start driving, ttyl

My phone buzzes on the dash, but I don't answer. Kennedy and Spencer talk so much shit together I would completely think they were in love with each other, but my brother has been happily married for over ten years. Kennedy fervently denies having any feelings for him. On the radio, I hear the familiar beginning beats of 8 *Days of Christmas*, by Destiny's Child, and turn the volume all the way up. Even though I sound like a duck mating call, I sing at the top of my lungs because this is one of my favorite songs. My birthday is October eighth, so I think it's my lucky number. Come to think of it, today is the eighth of December, and there are two eight in my new number. *Lucky indeed.*

Dad is already there when I pull up to my house, but he only lives ten minutes away, so it makes sense. It's pretty late, so I know there's only one thing he wants at this time of night–Dessert. Stepping out, he asks, "How you doing, Niecy?" The only person I let call me Niecy is Dad. Nyshon didn't even spell it right.

I run into his back when he walks into the house. His head swivels side to side, looking around like Kendrick did when he came over.

"I'm good, just trying to figure out how to manage all of this." Hanging my coat, I turn on the lights and click the remote to activate the lights.

"I see." Once I close the door, he turns around and asks, "Um, are you doing alright?"

"Why'd you ask that? I'm fine."

"Because your house... Shanice, why does your house look like Christmas threw up in here?"

"It's that bad?"

"Baby, did you put up every decoration Mom left you? Your Ma used to pick a theme and go from there."

"It's too much, I know. I'm just a little overwhelmed with everything. I'll figure it out though, eventually."

"I know you will. I had to come lay eyes on you after that message earlier. Now, what happened that you had to change your phone number? Is it that man your mama wanted you to leave?"

"He crossed the line, Daddy," I admit. "There was more to why we broke up, but I'm trying to move on, which meant I had to change my number. It sucks, but it is what it is."

"But you're safe?"

"I'm safe, Daddy. Worse comes to worst, I'll get Spencer on him."

"Alright, Niecy." Rubbing his stomach, he says, "Now, you know why I'm really here. Where's my desserts?"

I laugh, then direct him into the kitchen to load up a to-go plate. Sometimes, I need my daddy to bring me down to level zero, and he does it without even trying.

Chapter 15

Kendrick

"Morning, boss man!" Marshall is way too cheery today. Walking past his desk he holds open a stack of envelopes up for me to take.

"You gone through these yet?" Holiday cards are a waste of company resources. The postage itself is damn near a dollar.

"What do you take me for, an amateur?" he questions. "Two of them had phone numbers in them and were personally signed, so I threw those away first, but the rest are good for your revi—"

The cards are in his trash before he can finish his thought. If there's nothing important there, they can go. Marshall sends out e-cards on my behalf. At least those can be discarded without affecting the environment.

"Hey, before you go bah-humbug in your office, are we meeting tonight since Wednesday is going to be the next event?"

That reminds me... "Hey, were you able to get the committee on board for the last two events? If I have to be forced into this, they can at least do something for the community."

"Yup, they just confirmed. BuildBeyond suddenly had an open spot when I mentioned your name." Muttering, he says, "Go figure." But he knows I volunteer there all the time. "They also volunteered their kitchen for gingerbread baking with the kids in the women's shelter."

"I appreciate you, man."

Whispering he asks, "We working on that project tonight? The one for you know who."

"Man, you don't even know her."

"Yeah, but I get to meet her on Wednesday. And technically, I email her too."

I ask, "Why don't you have your glasses on?"

"Hmm... Touchy subject, huh?"

"Sometimes you're wise beyond your years. Other times you're just childish."

"I'm 27, not 18."

"Sure, you are... I'll be in my office." I close the door behind me, pull out my phone, and sit. In the thread between Shanice and me, the bubbles are still green. I tried to text her yesterday, but the message said, 'not delivered. '

I debate what I should do while thrumming my fingers on my desk. Do I say she got sick and couldn't come? Do I say we broke up? Ugh, I wish she would have communicated rather than just blocked me out of nowhere.

And what did I do? I thought things went well. I know I'm not supposed to care that much, but something deeper is growing between us, and I thought... I thought she felt it, too. Collab pings on my laptop, pulling me out of my thoughts and actually making me laugh.

Marshall: Clark Kent time, glasses are on.

Marshall: Heard you laugh. Victory!

Me: Yeah, yeah

Me: On second thought, we might not have to work on the other project tonight

Marshall: What the... omw

Marshall opens my door without bothering to knock. "What happened? Why aren't we working on it?"

"Because she blocked me," I mumble.

Eyebrows raised, Marshall says, "Come again? Why didn't you mention that a few minutes ago?"

"Maybe I wasn't ready to admit it."

"I *told you* to lay off the Christmas hate shit, Kendrick! I didn't even get a chance to meet her yet. So, what are you going to do about this?"

"There's nothing I *can* do about it. I'm not about to start cyber stalking her."

"You mean to tell me you didn't exchange MyGram pages with her?"

"Why are you acting like you don't know me all of a sudden?" *I hate social media.*

"You know, some days I think there's hope for you... and other days, you prove you're old."

Unable to stop the laughter bubbling out of me, I say, "Man, get the fuck out of my office."

"For real, did something actually happen?"

"Honestly, nothing happened. Well, not nothing, but everything went great. I truly don't know what I did."

"Alright, well then, don't trip. I'm sure she'll clear it up. We'll still work on this tonight, even if she doesn't get access, because it's also helping with my coding. Plus, I see a silver lining?"

"What's that?"

Before he exits my office, he smiles conspiratorially and says, "You care."

I do. A whole lot more than I should.

Hours must have passed before I looked up because Marshall had a coffee for me.

"You went to the shop by my house?" I ask.

"Please, I don't like you that much. I got delivery though. Let's get to it."

Two cups of coffee later, we are still stuck. Well, he's stuck. "But I don't understand why it's not working. We looped the code twice."

I'm trying to let him figure it out, but the urge to help is right at the tip of my tongue. "Have you—"

"Don't tell me, Kendrick! I'm going to figure it out," he grumbles while working his way through the code again, but he's not actually reading it. That's what's fucking him up.

"Okay, well stop whining about it and just think. You know the answer to this. Put the fucking coffee down and read the code. You're only looking at it."

"I've been reading the damn—oh shit." He finally sees what I see. This is the annoying part of mentoring because I just wanted to fix the shit for him, but he has to do the work.

Marshall types like a madman while mumbling to himself, "Stupid fucking error in the code got copied over. Now I gotta fix it in all the spots."

There are six places he needs to fix. But he's got this. While he's taking care of that, I check my phone and see a message from an unknown number.

> unknown: Hey, I didn't get details for tomorrow yet.

Staring at my phone I'm confused until the lack of communication clicks... She changed her number.

> Me: I sent the information but apparently, I've been talking to a brick wall

> unknown: oh shit, I'm so sorry Kendrick. I had to change my number. My ex is a psycho.

> Me: The one who sent you the flowers?

> unknown: OMG! Yes, he's nuts and kept calling me but now he can't anymore *upside down smile*
> Please send me the information again!

I overwrite her phone number and then copy and paste the information I sent yesterday.

"What you over there smiling for?" Marshall asks.

"Figured out the Shanice problem. She changed her number. She didn't block me."

"Nice. It's a good thing we just fixed this!"

After a few tests, we are at a good place to stop. I wait for Marshall so that I can take him to the train station. It seems like the day is finally starting to look up.

The next evening, when I pick Shanice up, the air is thick and tense, but she keeps saying she's okay. I even left the holiday station on for more than ten seconds to see if she would crack a smile, but she completely ignored it—so, of course, I turned that shit off. If she doesn't want to listen to it, I damn sure don't.

"How was work today? You had that meeting, right?" I ask.

"It was good. The Richard's assistant gave me a great idea of their style and tastes, but I'm nervous doing this by myself. It's a lot of house."

"Why would you be by yourself?"

"Well, as a junior designer, I'm responsible for the initial mockups. I'm nervous because this is the first time my new boss will be seeing something from me. Sure, he's seen my notes in other files, but this is like my first little baby."

"I remember when I first started, but I don't think you have anything to worry about. I'm not your boss, but if your designs at work are anything like the algorithms you've created for your website, you're going to knock that shit out of the park."

"Thank you." Her voice is soft and uncertain, but I want her to live in that sexy-ass confidence at work like she does outside of it. "What are we doing tonight again? I forgot. I'm sorry."

"No apologies necessary. We're going to be in the men's shelter tonight. There's about eighty of them. We have to set up the dining room first, and then we'll serve. Once the men have eaten, we'll be able to sit with them and talk."

"Is there anything I shouldn't say?"

"The coordinator will go over all of that, but if they are quiet, they don't wanna talk. I would talk to them like regular people instead of about their circumstances. Who the hell really wants to talk about their downfalls in life?"

She mumbles, "I sure as hell don't."

As we approach the facilities, she looks around wearing a mask of happiness. I don't like it, but this isn't real, so what can I say about it? After I park and help her out of my truck, one of the residents spots me.

"Kendrick, I didn't expect to see you here. How you doing, sir?"

"I can't call it, man. Look, tonight is a huge deal for me," I fake whisper because he loves the dramatics. "I have to impress this lady. She's way out of my league, so make me look good."

"Yeah, man, I can see that. She got that big hair like Diana Ross".

Shanice fluffs her hair and laughs, "Big hair, big secrets."

"I like this one. That other one never came with you to volunteer."

"Not every apple is ripe, ya know?"

With a thoughtful expression, he says, "Nah, not really, but you got it, youngin'. That's too far for my old tinker to think. Gone head inside and say hi to Bill. He'll be happy to see you. Merry Christmas, Son."

I shake his hand and then walk into the building.

"Are you going to ignore everyone that wishes you a Merry Christmas?" Shanice asks. When I don't answer, she waves her hand in front of my face. The bell on her bracelet jingles as she jokes, "Earth to Kendrick."

"Sorry, Bells."

Smiling, she says, "That's a new one. I kinda like it."

"Well, you said you hate Sweets."

"And do! Don't be such a grump, though. Just say 'same to you'. It's not gonna kill you."

I stutter step, and grab my chest, giving my best Fred Sanford impression. She's alarmed for only short seconds before she smacks my arm. "Jerk."

"You never know what'll happen. Let me be me, girl."

She smacks her lips and enters the facility. "Whatever, I'm gonna go see how I can help in the kitchen." As she's walking away, Marshall intercepts her and winks at me. She throws her head back with laughter at whatever he says, and it pisses me off instantly. When he wraps his arms around her shoulders, I want to knock his fucking head off, but I know that he's doing this to mess with me because I shouldn't care, but dammit, I do. *Asshole.*

Having her here with me means a lot more than she knows. Gran said the test of a person's character isn't how much they give but how they act when they serve. I'm curious to see how the residents respond to her. Her personality is so warm and charming. It's the little side glances and the way she scrunches up her face when she is about to call me out on my bullshit. One thing I know for sure is that Gran would have loved her, and she would have kicked my ass if I let her get away.

Chapter 16

Shanice

"Did you know Kendrick organized this whole thing?" Marshall is Kendrick's assistant, and I can tell he's one of those people that it's hard not to fall in love with. He's so sweet and kind, but he has a lot of charm and will talk the coat off your back if you're not paying attention.

"Hmm, he said that you were the one who planned all of this, so that's interesting."

"Well, he had the idea. I'm definitely the mastermind, though. I'm also helping on your website." His index finger touches his lips, and he whispers, "But that's our secret." I didn't realize Kendrick told anyone about our deal, but I told Kennedy, so it's not like I don't have someone to talk about this experience with. I guess I didn't expect it to be his assistant.

While Kendrick isn't around, I ask, "So, what are his friends like? He talks about his siblings a lot, but not friends."

"Oh…" He pauses for a moment, and his mouth twists to the side. "Outside of them, I probably claim the best friend label, but even that's a stretch."

"Any embarrassing stories you can fill me in on?"

I jump when a warm, firm body steps behind me and wraps his arm around my waist. His words are loud enough for us both to hear, but his breath against my ear makes goosebumps rise across my skin. "None that won't get him fired."

Marshall scoffs, "You couldn't fire me if you tried."

"Yeah, yeah."

With my apron on and hair pulled back, I'm ready to do what I can. Instead of the foods I imagine being served at a shelter, we're plating a catered meal. The residents seem so appreciative. Most of them acknowledge Kendrick in some way. He hides within himself during all the praise, but he deserves his flowers if he personally affects these people. Most of us here only do this because it's a Christmas event, but I can tell he is a regular based on their excitement seeing him.

Mom always talked about coming here to serve, and I'm happy to be able to live out that dream.

"Well shit, Kendrick graced us with his presence during Christmas? I'll be damned," an older resident says. I scoop some dressing onto his tray, and Kendrick adds the cranberry sauce.

Being nosey, I ask, "Oh, so he comes the rest of the year?"

"Mmm hmm, Bells."

"That's a good man," the resident says, pointing.

"He sure is." I place an impromptu kiss on his lips.

He deepens it, then winks and continues serving with a smile. He might not like the consumerism of holidays, but he likes giving. Even if he doesn't realize the connection, he does.

All evening, I learn the life stories of veterans, fathers, retired businessmen who can't make ends meet, and some who nobody bothers to check in on. It's an enlightening, sobering evening as I realize my own privilege. I hear more stories about Kendrick and how long he's been volunteering here. Overall, I'm having a great time fulfilling one of Mom's dreams, so I'll call it a success.

When we leave, I don't fight Kendrick on his offer to take me home.

"Thanks for driving me home." I hold Kendrick's hand as he walks me to my door. It feels nice to be holding his hand without anyone around.

"Oh, I should be the one thanking you. You know, you're not too bad."

I nudge him away a little. "Please, I'm the best thing that's happened to you all year."

"Yes, yes you are."

My breath catches in my throat. He moves closer and places his hand on the back of my neck. "I really want to kiss you, just as me and you."

Meeting him in the middle, I lean on my tiptoes, and our mouths crash together on my front porch. The chemistry between us burns hot and wild as we melt into each other. Neither of us wants to let go, but my nosey-ass neighbor picks that exact moment to holler out her window.

"Take that inside the house, child!"

Nose to nose, we laugh. It's just like her old lonely, seventeen cats having ass to get in the middle of my fun.

"And what happened after that? You fucked his brains out... that's the only acceptable answer, by the way," Kennedy says as we walk through the park.

Wednesday was so much fun. Seeing a different side of Kendrick made me see him as less of a grumpy holiday hater. "Cat lady interrupted us."

"*See*, I told you there was something I ain't like about that lady, but I ain't gone say I told you so."

"You just did, Kennedy."

"Well, I ain't gone say it again."

"Whatever, woman."

"You start cleaning up the house of chaos yet?"

"Hey! That's mean! I'm doing the best I can."

"Well, your best might not be good enough in this one instance. You need some dick that's not motorized, but you're not getting fucked anytime soon in that house of yours."

"Rude."

"Delusional," she counters.

"Heifer."

Kennedy takes a calming breath and then says, "I'm going to be the mature one and not let this keep going. Because if you go to hell I'ma have to meet you there." She purses her lips, but I know what she means. Kennedy will always tell the truth, but she also knows I'll keep going, which is almost always too far. It's a defense reflex. I'm healing, but not healed. It's hard to snap out of it sometimes. "So, what about work? How'd that go this week?".

"I don't deserve you," I admit.

She winks and I finally respond to her question. "The new job is so good, and it annoys me."

"I'm confused..."

"Me too, bitch. I'm happy, but I don't know how to feel about that. There's some bittersweet feelings. I'm gonna learn as much as I can in the meantime, but I want to be sure that I earned this."

"I feel that, and I'm proud of you, sis. Trust me, you deserve this." She gives me a side hug, and we keep walking in silence for a little bit. "Anything else from dumbass?"

"Girl, nah, hopefully my number change is enough. I wasn't joking. I will tell his wife, but I'm not tryna come to nobody as a woman at thirty-five."

Kennedy bends forward, laughing. "Bitch, I'm sick of you."

"Girl, I'm sick of me too. What's going on with you? How's Khalil?"

"Now, you know damn well I ain't got in contact with that man again."

"Why not, though? You didn't explain why you would be avoiding him after—and I quote— "The best sex you've had all year.""

She smacks her lips, then kicks a rock on the ground. She doesn't want to answer this question, which means I already know the answer. With a shoulder nudge, I encourage her to speak.

"He's too much. I don't know. It's like, it was a great night, but what the fuck do I do with that? Call him the next day? Arrange a date or something? Get married? Been there, done that. If I bump into him again, who knows."

Kennedy's been through a lot. I complain about what, he who shall not be named did, but Darrion was entirely abusive to her. She cut off contact with me for a few years at his request. I was pissed, but that's my baby, so when I got an out of the blue text with her location with the word help, I flew across the interstate. My bestie was on the side of the road, barely breathing. I can't tell her how to heal. I can't tell her how to grow, but I'm for damn sure going to be supportive if she makes that next move.

"What's your plans for the weekend?" I ask to fill the silence.

"Maybe I'll watch a few movies. Isn't that what you and Mama Nessa did every Sunday in December? Y'all picked a Christmas movie out of a jar, right? Did you pick?"

"I didn't pick a movie. It felt weird to do it alone."

"Your brother and dad don't want to? I'll come by if you want. I can—"

"No, it's okay. They're dealing in their own way. Dad said he wanted to be alone, and Spencer is working. I can deal with it on my own. Maybe I'll start a new tradition. Who knows?"

"You don't have to heal alone, Shanice. You have people. Call me if you change your mind. I don't have anything planned." At the corner where we part ways, I hug her to express everything I don't think I can put into words without bawling.

She squeezes my fingers tighter and holds me just as close before pulling away. "I'm serious. Call me if you need me."

Tears flow into the bowl of popcorn on my lap as I suffer through this movie. I suggested we meet up, but Dad went off into the abyss of grief, and Spencer had to work. That left me, myself, and I alone. Again. I could have called Kennedy, but she has her own family, and as much as I love them and know they mean well, I can't answer "How are you doing?" In that pitying tone, another fucking time.

Bitch, how do you think I'm doing? I'm alone. My mom is gone, and I'm still checking myself at the doctor to make sure I'm not in the ground next. The thing about having cancer is that you never feel free. Sure, you get to ring that bell, but this disease reminds you that you don't actually own your life. Your body is a rental vehicle for your soul, and whenever God decides it's time to snatch that motherfucker out, it's gone. I wipe the lone tear sliding down my cheek. *I'm such a crybaby, I annoy myself.*

My first Christmas movie of the year should be happier. The 8 Dates of Christmas is my absolutely favorite cheesy rom-com. I lean forward on the couch, hugging my pillow, and repeat the lines with the actors. "Baby I want you to meet me under this same mistletoe every year and every year I want you to remember that I love you just as much as the last time we kissed in this spot. I wanna wake up to you every morning and fall asleep next to you every night."

True love is hard to find and takes work to keep. What I like about this movie is that they didn't go off and get married right away. It ended with them being happy and together. Not every happily ever after looks the same, but I won't lie and say that I thought mine would come sooner than this. I'm not rushing it because good things take time. I've had the worst luck with men.

The timer on the oven beeps, and my mouth waters and I hobble to the kitchen. I've been sitting here too long, so one of my feet has fallen asleep, but I'll be damned if this feeling of pins and needles is going to make me burn my cookies. Steam pours from the stove door, and the warm smell of eggnog cookies fills the kitchen. Cinnamon, ginger, and nutmeg are the perfect smells for Christmas. As they rest on the counter, I whip up the cream cheese frosting and think about Kendrick. I haven't heard from him in days, but I haven't texted him either. I grab the homemade eggnog from the fridge to add to the frosting and dip my spoon in to taste test. *Mmmm, this is so fucking good.*

Instead of adding rum to the batter, I took both shots with no regrets. Mom would love these. She was the one who taught me to cook and bake and respect my kitchen. Once I'm done frosting the cookies, I sprinkle cinnamon sugar on top and snap a pic to send to the family chat. Kennedy isn't exactly family, but she balances the masculine energy.

Me: Aren't you jealous you didn't come now? Eggnog cookies :)

Dad: Ooh, save me some of those if you really love me.

12: the frosting is uneven

Asshole. But I've got something for his ass.

Me: So's your hairline…

Kennedy: *Spitting out drink gif*

Kennedy: Save me some, boo :D

Dad: Ha! Good one, baby.

The soft crunch of the exterior makes me groan while the flavors of Christmas roll over my palate. It's perfect. I lick my lips and an unexpected saltiness makes me look at the cookie, but it's blurry. *When did I start crying?* At some point, I have to heal, and now—when things finally turn around in my life—is the perfect time.

Chapter 17

Kendrick

"You lucky I didn't kill yo' ass for sitting in my chair."

Normally, the TV playing in the background doesn't bother me while I'm in the shower, but I hurry to rinse the soap out of my hair, so I can turn this shit off.

What the hell am I watching? Khalil sent me this dumb ass movie, and now I'm questioning why I ever listen to him. I wrap a towel around my waist and grab the remote. In my bed, I flip through cable because, for some reason, I still have it.

"Baby, I want you to meet me under this same mistletoe every year and every year I want you to remember—"

I flip through channels and turn to a broadcast, there's got to be a basketball game on somewhere. Romance books and movies are a farce, a happily ever after for those who can't experience it in real life. At one point, I thought I was living a dream, but I was fucking wrong. I should have known she was only in it for what she could get. The signs were all there. She kissed me whenever I said I love you but was ecstatic when she got gifts. She only wanted to stay at family events for a few hours but expected me to stay around her people all day. She adored Christmas, presents, and all the holiday things, so I thought it was the perfect time to propose.

Boy, was I wrong.

Buzz.

The doorbell buzzes, and I get up to find out who it is. Nobody texted me and said they were coming over, but only a few people know where I stay.

Pressing the button, I say, "Yo."

"Open up, less attractive twin."

I chuckle and let him up. After pulling on some shorts and a shirt, I take my time putting lotion on. When he comes to the door, I leave it locked. The doorknob twists back and forth a few times before he finally realizes it's not opening.

"Ayo, open the door, G. What you on, man?"

"What *you* on? Didn't nobody tell you to bring yo' bump head ass over here."

"Bruh, open the damn door!" He yells from the other side, knocking way too hard. "I'm about to start actin' real westside out here."

I see him turn around through the peephole like he's about to start kicking backward. Not wanting to disturb my neighbors with his bullshit, I unlock the door.

"Better had," Khalil mumbles, shoulder-checking as he enters.

"Whateva." I laugh.

He picks up the lotion on the side table and grins. "Aw, did I mess up your special alone time?"

Choosing to ignore him, I pull out my green box, then sink back into my comfy spot on the couch. Even though my brother's job makes him more money than mine, he still tries to "borrow" green from me, but he never brings any with him. Talkin' about I should have shared that settlement money with him because nobody actually knows if he got hit by a mail truck or me? He takes the identical twin part too far sometimes, and that's why people don't take him seriously. Even if I don't say it out loud, his antics don't do a good job of hiding his feelings—it makes them more noticeable.

"What's good with you, bro?" I twist the grinder, and I listen as he talks about his long-ass day and how he hasn't been able to contact Kennedy.

"Ayo, shorty was her friend, right? The one who was emailing you, and you wouldn't shut up about her. What was shorty name again? Shante? Sade?" he says, snapping his fingers.

"Shanice. Her name's Shanice, and no, you can't have her number."

He clicks his tongue and then sits back on the couch. "Just call her bro. Video call her so she can see how heartfelt I am."

"You ain't never been heartfelt."

"My dick was heartfelt after I left her friend."

"See, that's that bullshit I be talkin' about. Just admit she piqued your interest. Wasn't you at her house? Just go knock on the door or something."

"G, it was still dark when she 'suggested' I go home. What was I supposed to do? Take a picture of her address?"

I snort from his use of finger quotes.

"You coulda dropped a pin or something."

"Shit, I ain't even think of that. I gotta start thinking like the tech nerd."

He sits forward and grabs the remote from the coffee table, muting the TV. "Come on bro, just call her. It's not like I'm tryna pop up at her house or nothing."

"You needy as hell, you know that, right? Pass me my phone."

"Yes!" He exclaims and gets what I ask. "You're the best brother I have."

"Fool, I'm the only brother you have." I open the contact card and decide whether to video call her or give her a heads-up.

"Don't be a bitch. Just press the button." He scoots closer, but I angle away from him.

"I'll show you a bitch. There's a mirror right over there." While pointing to the hall mirror, I smile at my comeback.

"It'll still be your face," Khalil says, smirking.

Unable to contain my laughter, I send off a text.

> Me: Hey beautiful, you free right now?

Only a few minutes pass before my phone vibrates on my lap.

> Shanice: A hey beautiful text. How original.

Laughing, I start typing out a response.

"Is that her? Did she text you back?" Khalil puts weight on me to pull me backward.

I shrug him off and move over. "Man, you actin' real fuckin' thirsty right now." He huffs, and I answer her message.

> Me: I'm not even on that kinda time. I just wanted to call you real quick.

> Shanice: oh ok

> Shanice: I'm free.

I'm surprised by her radiance when she answers the call. Beauty isn't hard to find but like— I don't know. Her aura is so pure.

"Damn, you didn't say a video call."

"My bad, my bad. What you on?"

As she walks around her kitchen putting things away, I realize her phone is in that propped-up thing.

"Cleaning my kitchen. I made some cookies earlier."

"Oooh, what kind of cookies?" My mouth waters thinking about that soup I had of hers.

Khalil horribly whispers, "You gonna ask her or nah? I'm not about to sit and watch you flirt."

"Sorry about that, one second." After making sure to press mute, I angle in his direction. "Have you lost your mind? Don't fuck up my shit cuz you ain't got it."

Khalil raises his hands in defense. "My fault bro, I ain't even tryna do that to you. My fault."

After unmuting, I apologize, "Sorry about that, Khalil over here being thirsty. He wants your homegirl number, but I'm already knowing he not getting it. What kinda cookies you make?"

"Hey!" He says, dejected.

"Mmm hmm." She hums while sliding the apron over her head. "I made eggnog cookies."

"What's the likelihood you'll bring me some of them?"

"Tonight?"

"Yeah, tonight. It's the weekend. Nothing wrong with two friends hanging out."

The corner of her mouth tilts when she asks, "And why can't you come get some yourself?"

"Your house gives me nightmares. No offense."

She pouts. "I don't feel like driving."

"I'll send a car. No driving needed."

"I'll send a car." She mocks, "Where you live, up north?"

Khalil chokes when taking a sip of water.

"*Ooor*, and just hear me out; you can bring the cookies and whatever leftovers you don't mind sharing, and I'll watch a movie with you."

Her eyes brighten. "A Christmas movie!" It comes out more like a statement than a question.

"Good try. Look, why don't you invite your homegirl over, too, and we can all just chill for a little bit."

"Not in this tiny ass apartment," Khalil says under his breath.

Without fully turning to my brother, I respond to his comment. "You can leave."

"Damn, you being mean already?" She asks, smacking her lips.

"Shit, I was talkin' to Lil ass. He getting on my nerves, bein' thirsty for your friend."

"Yeah, she wouldn't come no way if he's there," Shanice says, factually.

Khalil sits back in his seat. "You not even gonna ask for me?"

"I'm sorry. I asked her about you earlier. In all fairness, she did say you put it down. She just..." her words trail off. "Her story isn't mine to tell, but yeah. I'm still not convinced about bringing you cookies."

"That's no fun." I pout on my side of the screen, but I doubt it makes a difference.

Her voice softens, and she grabs the edge of the sink. Her head drops as she says, "Sorry, I'm just not in the best mood today."

Leaving Khalil on the couch, I get up, walk to my room, and close the door behind me. "Gimme a second."

As fast as I can manage, I open the box of the little selfie stick thing, lengthen it on my nightstand, and then insert my phone. It doesn't take me long to get it set up, but tears pool in her eyes when I'm back on the camera.

"What's going on?" I ask.

"I don't know." She squints and leans forward into the camera, "Did you get a phone stand?"

"Work smarter, not harder, baby. You already teaching me things." Though she's trying not to smile, she can't help it. I've done my job. "Now, for real, tell Daddy what the problem is."

"Ugh, don't refer to yourself in third person or call yourself daddy."

"For real girl. I got listening ears."

"But your brother—"

"My brother is a grown man who can occupy his time for a few minutes while we talk. All he gone do is smoke some of my weed."

A loose curl falls into her face, and she exhales forcefully to blow it away. Since that didn't really help, she pulls the hair thing off her wrist and then confines her curls to a loose ponytail on top. Biting her lip, she says, "Maybe this is a convo for in-person… I'll bring some cookies."

"Bring your fine ass over here."

"Khalil not going to mind?"

Closer to the phone, I say, "Girl, I'll kick him out before I let him make you uncomfortable."

She loads a Tupperware container full of cookies. "Text me your address. I'll Maps it."

I shake my head. "I'll send you a pin. See you soon."

Chapter 18

Shanice

I've smelled myself approximately eighty-two times because I'm sweaty and nervous, but I showered before I left, so thankfully all I smell is cocoa butter. I've been around him in person before, but that was before we agreed to fake date, and way before I realized my feelings aren't fake. If I'm being honest, they never were. This creates another layer that probably shouldn't exist. He's become such a good friend to me, and despite his obvious cynical nature, he's still caring and charming and thoughtful, and I'm completely fucked. Kennedy was right, I do fall faster than her grandma.

"Turn left into the parking lot." I don't come to residential parts of downtown Chicago like that, so the GPS comes in handy—except in lower Wacker Drive. *If I end up down there alone, I'll never find my way out.*

I love my quaint little house, but I can't lie and say I haven't always wanted to live in a high rise at least once. I've asked myself twenty times on the way here if I was really going to open up to him, but I need to be able to talk to someone. If I talk to my family, they'll worry about what's happening. If they worry, I'll pull back.

I want to heal. I know hoarding decorations and pretending to be jolly when I'm broken isn't healthy, but talking to my therapist about this isn't helping. She understands the premise of grief and how the cycle ebbs and flows. But in our last appointment, she admitted she hadn't lost anyone close to her yet, so in some things, she doesn't know how to help. *Note to self: look for a new therapist.*

Most of the time, I'm reeling back when expressing my feelings because I hate the pitying look on their faces. And then there's the 'cycle of life' snide comments. Bitch, I know everybody dies, but I didn't expect my mama to be the first person I was grieving. I pray that no one treats them the same way when they lose someone close to them, but then again, karma is a dirty motherfucker sometimes.

Kendrick didn't know my mama, but he understands that grief is a journey. He understands how a scent, or a sound, or even having to think about someone in the past tense is painful. I want to be able to express my own feelings without being worried about triggering my dad, my brother, or even Kennedy.

I find myself wanting to learn more about him and not just the surface-level bullshit. Sure, we've talked a lot over the last few weeks, but you can only learn so much about a person from texts. I want to know why volunteering is so important to him. Why does he talk about his grandma and siblings but not his parents? I want to know *him.*

Like I spoke him up, Kendrick calls.

"Hey, you here yet?"

"Yep. Do I have to park somewhere special? You said to go into the lot, but where? Since when do apartment buildings have parking lots?"

"Trust me, we pay for it. I'm down here. I'm assuming you're the only one in the lot right now. Come to the front. We gotta put this sticker on your window."

"Ohh, does this give me access to park here anytime I want?" When I drive around the horseshoe entrance of his building, I can see him walking out, shaking his head.

His smile is bright when he comes to the window. "Nope, I only got a day pass. Anything more than that is a hassle."

I hang up the phone and roll down my window to rest my forearms on the window frame. "You saving that for your girlfriend?"

His nose is a few inches from mine when he answers. "My sister has it, but I make everyone else find parking on the street, including Khalil."

"Ooh, does that make me special?"

"Everything about you is special."

I look down so he can't see the heat blooming on my cheeks. When I look back up, he's smiling like he knows what I'm feeling.

Rather than make me feel uncomfortable, he jokes, "But if you tryna be my girlfriend, just say that. Aye, that's them cookies smellin' like that?"

He tries to reach over my lap to the container, and I swat his hand away. It grazes my thigh as he pulls back, but what I really want is to feel his hands on my bare skin. He hands me the sticker and says, "It's temporary so it comes off easy when you leave. Park in spot six. I'll be waiting for you inside the doors."

As he walks to the building, I pull up to the sign with the black six. I pull down the visor to take one more good look at myself. My cheeks are brighter, but my eyes are clear. That's an accomplishment after the last few days. Cookie container in hand, I drop my keys into my purse around my opposite arm and get out. My nerves jump around on the short walk to the door.

"So, this is where I live. There's the lobby. There's a small coffee shop that will be open in the morning that's decent. The gym is down that hallway."

He keeps pointing every little thing out until we get to the elevators. He's nervous. Aw, *that's cute as hell.* Apparently, we're getting into his favorite elevator of the two on this side of the building, but he likes the opposite one in the east elevators. Did I need to know this? Probably not, but it's fucking adorable and gives me a small glimpse into a different side of him.

On his floor, I easily spot his door. It's the only one not decorated for Christmas. His personality shines through with a mat that says, 'I'm not home'. That's hilariously on the nose. Through the now open door, I get a good look inside his apartment.

It's not modern at all, yet somehow, it still looks sterile and cold. Single male clients at our age usually have a bunch of mismatched furniture that are sentimental pieces. The futon from high school. The dresser they bought in their first apartment or Grandma's old dining table they ate at as kids.

Kendrick's is all new, and it matches perfectly, but none of it seems to match the vibe I get talking to him. As I turn toward the TV, his voice brings me back.

"Shanice, did you hear me?"

"Huh, what you say?"

His smile is knowing. *Ah shit*, he figured out what I was doing.

"Did my place pass the inspection?"

My cheeks heat as I shrink. "Sorry, you can take a day off work, but being an interior designer is in my every thought. I can't always help it."

"Oh, y'all are so cute." Whipping around, I see Khalil leaning over the back of the couch, resting his head on his forearms. I turn back around to Kendrick and shit, I forgot how identical they were.

"Hey, Khalil. How you been?"

He pats the cushion next to him. "Come on, sis. Let me get some of those cookies. I smelled them as soon as you came in."

Before I can respond, Kendrick stands in front of me and says, "Hell nah, if anybody is getting some of her cookies, it's me."

I pull my lips between my teeth to stop from laughing, and Khalil groans before falling back on the couch dramatically. "I'm going to call Kaliyah on you. You're being mean to me again."

"Man, I don't give a *fuuuck*. She likes me more anyway."

I stand, chuckling as they continue to bicker back and forth. Eventually, he turns and places both hands on my shoulders and twists me toward the kitchen, away from his brother.

His touch is firm as he slides his hands gently down my arms, where they rest on my hips. His thumb grazes the side of my bare skin, and I shiver. Either he knows how to moisturize his hands properly, or they're sweaty—which is a gross alternative. At the counter, he lets go, but I miss his touch.

"Remind me what kind of cookies those are again."

His hungry ass licking his lips, staring at the Tupperware.

"They're eggnog. At first, I was gonna add a rum flavor, but with the way I'm feeling, those ended up as shots."

"You need anything to drink?"

I didn't expect this level of hospitality, and I hope the surprise is not too obvious when I respond. "Oh, whatever you have is fine. I'm cool with anything."

"Fasho, because if you didn't drink milk with cookies, I was going to judge you."

What I don't expect is for him to go into the fridge and pull out a container of oat milk. I can't help the gag that forces its way up.

He whips around to check on me. "What happened? You okay?"

"That's not milk," I cringe.

"It's a milk alternative unless you wanna smell the effects of lactose intolerance all night."

Ew. "Ya know, I could have gone my whole life without knowing that."

He puts the notmilk on the counter and gets more defensive than I thought he would. "I told you we were friends, and I meant that shit. Don't be surprised by what I say."

I didn't expect hearing him say "friends" would be as much of a punch to the gut as it is, but here I am. If he's going to deflect his feelings, so am I.

"I think I'll go hang with Khalil out there, just in case." I walk toward the living room. He pulls me back firmly by my biceps.

I'm against the refrigerator when he leans down to talk in my ear. "I don't play that shit about my brother. We might share a lot of things, but you are mine."

He takes a step back, fills a cup of milk for himself, and winks before walking to the living room. "Come on bestie."

I'm feeling a myriad of things after that interaction. One—Kendrick could say omelet du Fromage, and I'd think it's sexy. Two—don't make anymore jokes about Khalil, that was a clear boundary. Three—I really, really like this man.

The only question now is, what am I going to do about it?

Chapter 19

Kendrick

I didn't expect Shanice to sit down and smoke with us. Where some people see smoking as unladylike, I love watching her cheeks hollow as she inhales and swallows down the smoke before releasing it into the air. She's this sexy, business savvy woman who clearly knows her shit and gets her money, but she also knows how to relax.

"Aye, did you know skittles are all the same flavor?" Khalil asks, holding his smoke.

Accepting the pass of the second in rotation from me, Shanice rejects that idea. "That's not what the package says. The pink ones are my favorite."

Blunt in hand, Khalil points to his forehead, "Nah sis, that's what they want you to think, but it was a whole thing on MyGram. You see, you said pink ones and not strawberry."

"You say that like we don't already identify Kool-Aid by the color. It's not cherry, it's red, same difference."

He shakes his head vigorously, then says, "Nah, nah, nah. So, I read those aren't actually different either though, and that's why we call it by the color cuz' we can't taste the flavor."

"What is you talking about right now?" I can't take it any longer because now he's going too far. "Yo' high ass needs to chill for a minute, Lil."

"What you mean? I ain't even say nothing." He sulks, sinking into the couch. "I didn't even get to talk about the Denver airport."

"The one with the secret tunnels underground that they allow aliens to transport through?" Shanice asks.

I can't help but smile as they go off on a high-ass tangent, yet again. We've gone through two blunts and nearly her whole container of cookies. I ordered some regular milk for her through the delivery, which made bro way happier than I realized it would. Khalil sang *Hallelujah* as they drank the intestine turner. Somehow the lactose intolerance skipped him. *Lucky*.

"And you're sure she won't talk to me?" Khalil asks as he leans against the opposite arm of the couch, cradling a pillow. The fuck is this? Girl talk? I'm in the middle of them, and to my advantage, she crosses her legs at the edge of the couch. They keep falling off because my couch isn't that deep, so I place her feet on my lap, rubbing in circles.

Her eyes meet mine as she responds, "Yeah, unfortunately so. She's the person you have to let fly until she's ready to relax. All you need to hope is that you impressed her enough for her to reach out when she's ready. If that time ever comes."

My chest rises as I watch her mouth move while she speaks. I can't help remembering that kiss. The one that had me coming harder against my hand in the shower than I have in a long time. The only thing that I know I'll enjoy more is being inside her.

"I'll be Santa if you wanna sit on my lap," Khalil says before I tune back into reality.

"The fuck you just say?" I snap.

He leans back. "Chill out. It was a joke. I was just tryna break you out of whatever that was."

Annoyed, I cut my eyes away. Shanice has her head back as I knead my knuckles into the balls of her feet.

"Ya know, I think I gotta water my plants. I'll come back to get my car in the morning." Khalil mumbles as he gets up to leave.

I don't take my eyes off her. "Bye."

Shanice waves as she hums appreciatively. The soft whoosh of my door and the click of the lock let me know Khalil is gone.

"*Fuck, Kendrick.*" She whispers so low that I can barely hear. I would pay any amount of money to hear her say that over and over again. Our eyes lock, and she admits, "My feet have been aching for days." She tries to pull her feet down, but I hold her ankles.

"I didn't forget about that phone call. What's going on?"

She leans up on her elbows and blows out air. "I'm regretting that I brought that up earlier."

"What's going on?"

This time I release her when she pulls away, tucking her feet beneath her. Her juicy thighs are pressed against the rips of her jeans, and my mouth waters. I wanna taste all of that, but I pull it together.

"I'm not sure if I'm doing right by my mom. She... She loved Christmas, and I want to keep her memory alive. Sometimes I feel like I'm losing myself in the process."

"That's 'cuz the decorations are fogging up your brain."

She pouts while side-eyeing me, "I'll leave if you're not gonna listen."

I pull her to my side. She rests her head on my shoulder and sighs. "I had ovarian cancer about five years ago." Her words come out stoically, like she's reciting the days of the week instead of telling me about something incredibly difficult that she's lived through. My stomach drops, and I squeeze her closer while she takes a break from speaking.

"It was the second-hardest thing I've ever had to work through. The week after I rang my bell, my mom passed out in the grocery store. We thought it was just exhaustion because we'd all been through so much over the years I was in treatment. My situation was... complicated, putting my whole family through the wringer. She got better after a week or so, but then, a few months later, it happened again. Apparently, she went to the doctor but didn't tell anybody she found out she had stage three kidney cancer. By the time she let Dad tell us, I had already noticed the weight loss, gaunt eyes, sallow skin, and the pure exhaustion she was always complaining of. One day, I confronted her. From there on, I took leave and went to every appointment with her and Dad. My brother Spencer is a cop, so he couldn't take as much time off, but yeah..." Her words trail off as she stares at the ceiling.

She had cancer. Her mom passed from cancer. I want to ask a million questions, but right now, she just needs to talk. That's why she came, after all.

"Mom left all of her Christmas stuff to me, but I'm not her, ya know. I didn't pay enough attention to how she set everything up, so everything I've done feels wrong. I can't come up with a theme or decide on colors. It's why everything is so chaotic. At least it feels the same as my brain."

My thumb runs circles on the side of her arm as she continues to talk about the pain of losing her mom. I don't like her talking like it's her fault, though.

"You're kind and thoughtful, strong and fierce. You're also stubborn as shit, but if your mom was anything like mine, I know she'd be proud of that too. Why do you think you're failing her for real? It has to be about more than decorations." I can't figure out the missing piece of the puzzle.

"Mom didn't like Nyshon, my ex. We were only together for like six months, but she didn't trust him because he hated Christmas. And she had this thing about hating holidays being a red flag of unhealed trauma."

Ouch. That one struck a nerve. Her words trail off, but I'm trying to wait to speak until I know it's the end. I have a feeling she doesn't talk about her emotions much.

"I thought she was trippin' and ignored her. In the end, she was right, and the last argument we got into before she died was because she asked me to leave him before she passed. She wanted to see me at peace, but I thought I was at peace *with* him."

I know my hold has tightened on her, but she's gripping my shirt like she needs to be close to me, too.

"My dad and brother think I left him to honor her wishes." Her voice is barely a whisper as she continues. "I left him when I found out he wasn't actually single, and I was unknowingly his side piece. Imagine me finding that out after we just had sex. It was mortifying. I haven't been able to bring it up to my dad and brother, but I feel like a liar. They think I left him because she asked."

"Sorry to hear that. Have you ever thought about it, like maybe your mom sent that revelation to you? Maybe you were having a hard time before because of trauma bonds, ya know? But her sign brought forth the info you needed to choose yourself."

"Clearly, I don't pick the right people."

"You say that like there's been multiple bad luck men."

Scoffing, she continues, "Oh, you have no clue. I was with the same man throughout my twenties. When Brandon finally proposed, I was the happiest person on the planet—until I wasn't. Like a switch flipped, he started getting abusive, but my therapist gets paid to listen to that shit. So yeah, there have been multiple. Sometimes, my mouth gets me in trouble. Even if he hit me, at least I got my words in, and I didn't care about the consequences. I know that I'm on the defensive too much, but I'm healing, not healed."

Resting my chin on her head, I look at the ceiling, trying to settle the rage. The only thing I hate more than liars are abusive people. There's no way I'd disrespect my partner like that.

"I don't want to say I understand what you've been through because I can't fathom it. My grandma was my favorite person in the world; all it took was one hug from her to make my day and settle my nerves. She passed away almost three years ago.

She lived a long, love-filled life, but there's never enough time. She despised my girlfriend, Rose, with every bone in her body, but I didn't get it—at first. I thought I found my wife, but I was wrong. She played the fuck out of me, but I realized her problems were her problems. Just like your ex, what he did wasn't your fault. You're worth more than whatever value you think he gave you."

She squeezes me tight, and I turn my head to place a kiss on top of her head. Instead of kissing her head in an innocent and caring gesture, she tilts her chin up to look at me, and my lips accidentally connect with hers. That wasn't my intention at all. I freeze, pulling away quickly with the intent to apologize, but she grabs my face and presses her tongue into my mouth.

"Damn girl," I whisper against her lips. She swings onto my lap. My hands grip her thighs, and I squeeze, making my index finger glide against the edge of her core. She jerks from the touch before she leans in a little and rolls against my hands.

I follow her lead to provide pressure with my thumb. She shivers and gasps. When she pulls away, her cheeks are blushing despite her brown skin. I unbutton her jeans and glide my fingers under her panties. She moans against my touch. Slowly, I insert my index and middle, waiting for any sign that she wants me to stop, but she rises on them to build a rhythm.

She tightens with every swirl of her hips, and I curl to reach for that soft spot behind the curve. As soon as I find it, her head falls back, and she quickens her pace.

"That's it, Bells. Take what you want."

I love it when a woman isn't scared to take her pleasure. Her wetness drips down my fingers, and I'm rock hard. My mouth waters as I think about how she must taste. I'm not letting another drop go to waste. If she's going to finish anywhere other than my dick, it's going to be on my face. Pulling my fingers out, I suck them into my mouth. She bites her lower lip, and the sound of her whimper makes my dick jump.

She tastes like cinnamon and cardamom, like Christmas cookies, and the berry sweet undertones of what we smoked. Her eyes linger on me with a heat that makes my chest tighten. Her desire radiates loud and clear as she stares at me with her lips slightly parted. I can't wait to fuck that throat of hers, but first, it's time for a meal.

Chapter 20

Shanice

I giggle as he yanks me down, and a feral sound rumbles within his chest. His tongue meets the inside of my ankle, and I still. Biting my lip, I wait for him. He pulls my pants down my legs while licking his lips.

Trailing kisses up my inner thighs, he nears the place that's *impatiently* waiting for attention. I don't expect him to bite my skin, but as his teeth meet my thigh, I get even wetter. He follows the bite with a gentle kiss, then dives in headfirst.

My God.

"Oh fuck, Kendrick."

He devours me. Most men attempt to lick in the general area, but he is thrusting his tongue inside of me. I would be lying if I said this felt anything other than amazing. Unable to help myself, I roll my hips against his face. He places his hands under my cheeks and pulls me even closer.

Swirling the flat of his tongue against my center, he murmurs, "This shit tastes so good, but I need some more space, Bells." I gasp when he hoists me off the couch. He places my legs over his shoulders and then pushes to his feet while maintaining the pace of his tongue strokes. I bounce against his face with every step down the hall.

Oh shit.

I writhe while holding his head. When he sucks on my clit, I can't help crying out, "Dammit, Kendrick."

I jerk against the tongue he's still torturing me with. His hands grip my ass for support as my climax rolls over me in waves. I can't see shit, but at this moment, I don't give a fuck about safety.

My stomach falls to my back when I'm dropped onto a bed. Kendrick licks the evidence of my arousal from around his mouth, smacking his lips like he just devoured a perfectly cooked steak. When he removes his shirt, I trail my eyes along the tattoos on his torso, and I see that thick and delicious dick through his boxers. *Damn.*

Nodding at my shirt, he demands, "Take the shit off," while grabbing a condom from the bedside table.

My T-shirt and bra fall to the floor, and I drop my legs open expectantly. *He ain't gotta tell me twice.* He groans and grabs me by the ankles, yanking me toward the edge of the bed.

My grip on the comforter tightens as I prepare for him to slam into me, but he's gentle and groans with every inch he inserts. His mouth meets my hardened nipples, and that magical tongue of his flattens and flutters, making my back arch off of his mattress. I appreciate his sensitivity, attention, and care, but it's been so long since I've been fucked. I just want to feel him. His hands grab onto my love handles as he fucks me senseless. *Finally.*

"Touch that clit. I wanna feel you come on my dick."

Like a good girl, I trail my hand down my body and rub circles on my clit. I feel him hitting places that haven't been touched in a while. What I don't expect is for his finger to use the lubrication from my arousal to gently push the tip of his finger into my ass. I don't always like back-door play, but he seems to know what he's doing, and I appreciate his gentleness. The dual pressure, along with the fact that I'm also rubbing myself to the edge, has me making some rough, loud, and nasty sounds. His finger curls, and just like that, I'm coming hard as fuck.

He lifts me on an angle to hit the deep spot where only Winston has been able to reach. I smile, and he pauses to bend down and lick my lips when another release is about to push me over the edge. My stomach muscles shake, and my legs buckle.

"Oh, you like that shit deep, huh, Bells?"

With every thrust inside me, he moans. "This feels so damn good girl." He thrusts harder and harder. "You takin' this dick like it's yours, baby."

I roll my hips in coordination of his movements, like a dance. "Yes, Kendrick. *Fuuuck, yes.*" My nails claw into his back as my body starts to convulse. When my core tightens, he buckles forward. His shoulders shake like he's balancing a boulder on his back and the sound leaving his throat is guttural and sexy. Careful not to land on me, he drops to his elbows and inhales rapidly.

The aftershocks of pleasure still run through me when he pulls out. Sweaty, I lay like a starfish. My body is spent and boneless. It should be illegal for men like him to exist.

A minute passes before he rises and heads to the bathroom, coming out with a damp towel to wipe me clean. Normally, I have to get up myself and waddle to the bathroom if I want to sleep dry, but here he is, making sure I'm good yet again—*without* me having to ask. This man is dangerous to my body... and somehow, he's started to heal another crack in my heart.

I'm worthy of aftercare. I'm worthy of pleasure. I'm worthy of whatever it is I desire.

I take a minute to pay attention to his room as I lay in his bed. There's so many opportunities to do something nice here. I wonder why he hasn't.

After taking care of the towel, he gets back into his bed and curls an arm around my waist to pull me closer. "You never told me what you think about my place." His after-sex voice is rough and sexy as fuck.

"Oh, uh, it's very well put together."

He tickles my side, and I instinctively stick my butt out and laugh.

"Aye, you keep pushin' that thing back here and I'ma put something in it."

Oop. "I'm trying to figure out where I said I wouldn't want that."

A firm slap stings against my ass, and he nibbles on my ear. "Tell me what you think, woman."

I can't help the soft moan that leaves my throat, but I respond. "It's warm and supposedly inviting. The pieces all match together and are super adult-like and responsible."

"But..." he prompts.

How do I say this without sounding like an asshole? I prop my arm under my head. "None of it actually seems like you. If I had to guess, this was the furniture that was staged in the apartment, and you just bought it because it looked nice." His smile falters with each word. I feel like a jerk. "But it's still really nice." The words come out quickly as I try to recover, but it's too late.

He sits up abruptly. I lean back and cover myself with the blanket. He pulls a shirt over his sculpted body, and my shoulders drop. I look around the floor for my clothes when he walks over to my side and places a kiss on my forehead. Okay... *now I'm confused.*

He has a branded work t-shirt that looks new in his hand. "Here, put this on. Let's go take a look at what I did with Marshall so far."

I put the shirt over my head and reach for my panties, but he blocks my hand and lets out a throaty and delicious chuckle.

"There's no need for those."

With a wink, he takes my hand to help me out of the bed and intertwines his fingers through mine to walk back into the living room.

He keys in a long ass fucking password on his laptop, then clicks a few buttons. Before I catch up to what's really happening, a beautiful website display is revealed.

"Oh my God." I make grabby fingers and reach for it.

Smirking, he scoots closer. "It's almost done, but let's test it out."

"Who am I going to test this out on? I haven't given you all of the external links yet. Speaking of, is this going to be something I can edit easily, or am I gonna have to keep bothering you?"

"Slow down, little mama. You weren't great with working your phone, but if I show you, I think you might be able to handle it. I won't mind you asking me to help either."

I roll my eyes. "That still doesn't explain who is going to test it. I'll just put myself in as a client."

He directs me to the client list. "I'm your first client. Pass it back to me. You calling my house boring. Let's see what your system says."

Now I'm scared as fuck. I didn't realize I would have access so soon. The concept for this website took me a year to develop. I'm still perfecting the algorithms and endpoints.

He moves through the prompts, answering the questions. He even does a second run-through to make sure he agrees with what's there before clicking proceed.

The browser arrow swirls until it comes to a broken link.

"Oh, thank fuck." I whisper.

I'm happy it isn't working because seeing a client's face when they see the choices my program gives them in front of them—I don't know if I'm ready for that.

His fingers fly over the keys, checking code after code until he highlights three that, for some reason, he knows are broken. Not going to lie, that was sexy as fuck. Like— sexy *as fuck*.

Initially, I was indifferent about him telling me not to wear my panties, but now I couldn't be happier. I place my hand between my legs and insert my fingers. His mouth drops open when he turns to me, the code long forgotten.

"You're unreal, you know that, right?" Moving the laptop onto the coffee table, he turns to me and kneels between my legs, stroking his tongue across my working hand and core. He moans and kisses my fingers and entrance. Leaning back, he watches as I pleasure myself. When my head falls back, he bends down and adds one of his fingers to mine. *Oh shit.* He twists and turns to reach places my hand can't, and it takes only a minute for me to fall over the edge.

Standing, he frees himself from his shorts. "Come show me if you're as good with your mouth as you are with your hands, Sweets."

Here he goes with this nickname again. "I liked Bells more than Sweets. Princess will do, too."

He hums, then curls his finger, beckoning me closer. "Now that I've tasted you, it's going to be hard not to call you Sweets, but bring that sexy ass mouth over here, Princess. Don't make me wait."

My pussy throbs as I move from the couch onto my knees in front of him. I dip my fingers into myself, then stroke his dick with the same hand before adding my mouth.

"Oh shit. You don't play fair," he moans, placing his hand on the back of my head. He grips my hair, and I swallow him down. My mouth waters so much it's dripping from the sides of my jaw. My hand glides easily, and I moan every time his length slides over my tongue.

"Damn, Shanice. Your mouth wet as fuck."

I grab his balls with my other hand, then add pressure behind them with my finger.

His knees buckle, but I keep sucking him into my mouth. He bites his lip and starts fucking my face. His eyes roll, then a saltiness sprays to the back of my throat.

Once his body stops quaking, I get up to swish some water around my mouth, but my phone rings. The siren makes it clear it's my brother. Kendrick brings it to me, and I take a breath to compose myself before answering.

"You took forever to pick up the phone. What if this was an emergency?"

Annoyed, I use the rebuttal he's ingrained in my brain. "If it was an emergency, you'd be dialing 911. What's up, Spencer?"

"Can we have breakfast tomorrow? I have the morning off, and the family is going to my in-laws."

He sounds unsteady, and I'm confused. "You're calling me this late to go to breakfast?"

Murmuring, he admits, "I want to talk about Mom and *maybe* go to the cemetery tomorrow. I don't want to be alone when I go."

Sighing, I pinch my nose. He definitely could have just said that. "I'll be there tomorrow morning; just text me the details so I can set a reminder."

With a pout, I turn back to Kendrick. His shoulders slump, and his jaws tighten. Lips pressed into a line, he holds back on whatever he wants to say for real. He stands tight, ready for the disappointment he could predict from what he heard.

"I should get going. My brother wants to meet for breakfast tomorrow, and I only sleep in my bed."

"But you can stay here with me..." His words trail off as he makes his wishes known. Brows drawn together, his eyes lose a little of their usual spark.

I hate that look on him, but I don't want to jump into this any faster than I already have.

"I don't want this to break me when it's done," I admit, barely above a whisper.

"You're not the only one who's been broken. Maybe it's time both of us heal instead of letting past pains steal our future."

"I can try," I whisper.

"That's all I need, Bells. Just give me a chance."

"You'll pick me up for the event tomorrow, right?" I ask.

"Just let me know what time, baby."

From the window, I start my car, then collect my clothes, strewn around to get dressed. When I try to hug him goodbye, he pulls his coat on and then opens the door. The walk down to my car is quiet. Inside my car, I give him a sad smile, but he leans in and places a soft kiss on my forehead.

"Night, Shanice. Text me when you get home at least, okay?"

I can't manage to say any words as emotions battle their way to the surface, but I nod. He closes the doors, puts his ungloved hands into his pockets, and then walks back into the building—out of sight. *Am I ready for the consuming relationship Kendrick is suggesting?*

With my sad girl playlist on, I spend the ride home wondering if I'm in over my head.

Chapter 21

Kendrick

"So, you're telling me y'all ain't fuck after I left? I call bullshit." Khalil asks the next afternoon. After dropping the best head I've ever had in my life, she left me praying for a replay.

"Is there anything else you want, or you really called me asking for an answer you know I'm not gonna give?"

"Man, you on that bullshit. I ain't ask for details. I just was tryna see if that tension was only me feeling it."

"We have strong chemistry, but we knew that before yesterday. That's all I'ma say. How's shit going for you?"

"It's all good, bro. Aye, you heard from Kaliyah in the last few days? She never called me back."

Looking to my left at my sister on my couch, she shakes her head, but I'm not getting in the middle of their bullshit.

"She's over here now, but she ain't tryna talk."

She smacks my arm. "Why you say that?"

"Man, whatever. I gotta come get my car anyway. I'm about to walk over there. I'm your sibling too!"

When I end the call, Kaliyah crosses her arms. "Why you say that to him? Now I'ma have to spend twenty minutes reassuring him that I love him. That boy got a lot of abandonment issues."

"Yeah, yeah. You're not helping either."

She smacks me again. "Don't yeah yeah me!"

"The hell you always hitting me for? Heavy-handed ass."

"Whatever, now tell me about this girl. Did you have sex?"

"Uhh, not you asking too. Y'all need to get outta my business. I'm a grown ass man, not a teenager."

Smirking, she crosses her legs on the couch. "Ooh, it was good then. Okay, come on, tell me more."

"Get the fuck outta my house."

Laughing, I stand to get some water. That shit was so good and not just because it's been a long time. Her pussy gripped my shit like she wasn't trying to let it go, and I damn near want to live in it.

"Come on—Details! You never tell me anything about your girlfriends."

"That's not going to change today because she's not my girlfriend." Yet.

It's silent for longer than I thought it would be. When I turn back to face her, her mouth is basically on the floor, and she's looking at me like I slapped her.

"Are you fucking kidding me? She has you out here cheesin' like a kid, and she's not your girlfriend. A,w hell nah, wait until Khalil gets here."

I sit on the couch and pull out my lockbox, but she smacks my hand, then takes my weed box and sits on it. She has to stop hitting me all the damn time.

"You're not smoking your way out of your emotions. Plus, you're driving me home, remember?"

"Wait a second, you never answered me on where the hell *you're* coming from?"

Her phone starts vibrating on the table. "Oh shit!" She's reading a message and clearly ignoring what I said because she's texting back. I snatch her phone from her hands, but she grabs for it and yells, "Hey, give that back!"

Reading her message, I see it's from her friend Ressa's crazy ass. 'Amira, I apologize for making you uncomfortable in a public setting.' *Damn.* Women are fucking brutal. It's all I can see before she snatches the phone back from me and points her finger in my face.

"Don't touch my phone, Kendrick. You're not my dad."

"I don't wanna be your dad. Now tell me where you're coming from."

She crosses her arms defiantly, and the buzzer sounds repetitively. With a smile, she says, "Khalil is here. Looks like this has to wait."

"Yeah, yeah. Whatever." I press the intercom button to speak. "We're coming down."

It doesn't take long to put our coats on and meet Khalil downstairs, but he complains anyway. "Damn, it took y'all long enough. First, you're hanging out without me, and now you're making me wait like somebody in your apartment still... wait... Is Shanice still up there? Did you meet her, Kaliyah?" Sticking his tongue out, he continues, "It doesn't matter because I met her first, and even if you met her before today, I met her the same day that he met her, so I'm the more important person. We even smoked together and everything last night."

Kaliyah snaps her head in my direction. I don't smoke with a lot of people. The last time that happened, I almost didn't make it home. "You let her smoke with you?"

"Yup! There was so much tension in there I thought they were going to start stripping in front of me. I don't wanna see him naked... but her–"

He doesn't get to finish that thought because I turn around and swing, but he predicts my fist and dodges. Kaliyah pops us both in the back of the head like we aren't her big brothers. "Khalil, stop starting shit with him. Kendrick, he couldn't have riled you up if you didn't have feelings for her, so just admit it and move on."

Taking the keys, she opens the door to my truck and makes Khalil sit in the crew cab. We fight over the music station because she wants to listen to the holiday jams station, and I would rather drink apple cider vinegar on an empty stomach.

"Why you gotta make everything difficult, bro? Just let her listen to the damn station."

"This is my fuckin' car. How y'all think you're gonna get in here and tell me what to do? I don't have to listen to cheesy ass Christmas music in *my* truck."

Kaliyah mumbles, "You make shit so hard now. I remember when that's all you used to play."

"Yeah, and I remember when Gran plugged it into my radio favorites every time I got a new car, but she can't do that anymore, can she?" I'm tired of them bringing shit up from when Gran was alive. She's gone, and after she passed, the person I loved turned down my proposal in front of everyone and left me for a bitch. She used me, and my dumb ass fell in love with her.

Khalil looks at me. "With all due respect, that shit ain't got nothing to do with nothing. I know how much you loved Gran and how much she helped you after the accident, but like... we all loved her. Mom and Dad didn't take advantage of you or your money. Gran wouldn't want you actin' like this, and I know that for sure."

"And how exactly would you know that?"

"Because she wrote us letters and told us the truth. You told us you were asking her to marry so quick after Gran passed because that's what she wanted you to do, but you're fuckin' lying. That's why we weren't supportive, but we knew it wasn't the time to bring it up."

Kaliyah nods her agreement while twiddling with her fingers.

I stare at him. Why would they wait until now to tell me they knew?

"We let you sulk because you needed to feel the pain after being numb the whole time. She was sick. Plus, you've gone the whole day without acknowledging that it's been three years today."

My hands grip the steering wheel much stronger than needed. I was trying *not* to harp on it. Mom and Dad already called me this morning, complaining that I've been ignoring them for weeks. I have, but it's because of this. I was hoping I would get a little normalcy with my siblings, for it not to be a reminder that she's gone. *Apparently, that was too much to hope for.*

Kaliyah's been quietly sitting next to me. "Mom and Dad have the girls, and you would know that if you stopped ducking and dodging their calls. I took a rideshare to your house. Khalil was supposed to be here as moral support. He actually thought that yesterday was the day because he's horrible with dates. That's why he popped up out of nowhere."

I'm quiet. This whole thing was a setup, but I still don't understand what it's set up for. Clicking off the ignition, I wait. Before I realized what I'm doing, I search the street for her car. The lights are off in Kennedy's house.

Kaliyah catches my stare and asks, "Why are staring at Kennedy's house like a creeper?"

Khalil looks around maniacally. "Where is she?"

Then, something hits me. "Wait, you said you didn't remember where Kennedy lives. You were not at her house." I needed this laugh.

Gasping, Kaliyah puts it together. "You fucked Kennedy?" Her laugh is obnoxious, but this is gold.

Khalil crosses his arms and scrunches his face up. "What's so fucking funny? Does she live over here or something?"

"Or something," Kaliyah says, still laughing. "You'll never know which house, though, because she rarely opens her front door."

"Whatever." Khalil huffs. "We have important things to talk about, though." The mood in the car shatters when he hands me a small envelope with Gran's handwriting. I use my keys to perforate the seal, pull out the single note card from her desk stationary, and turn it to face whatever words are there. *Trust.*

My eyes start to water, and I trace the curves of her mixed print and cursive writing style. I laugh, thinking of the last whooping she gave me when I was a kid. I tried to forge her signature on a permission slip for a trip we couldn't afford for me to go on.

"I have one too," Kaliyah says, reaching into her purse. It's another envelope. My name is scrawled on the front of this one as well. Inside is another index card with another word. *Live.*

Well, that's easier said than done. If all it took to live a fulfilled life was writing it on an index card, she'd still be here.

Chapter 22

Shanice

I'm at the coffee shop where Spencer wanted to meet. The weather dropped like ten degrees, and it's a cold ass day to be outside. I rub my hands together to warm up. Spencer raises his hand, and I approach the booth in the back and sit down across from him.

"I ordered your bagel and hot chocolate already."

I give Spencer a hug and then have a seat. "Thanks, I appreciate you."

The silence is awkward, but honestly, since Mom died, I haven't seen much of my brother. It looks like neither of us have a healthy outlet for our grief. Not wanting to sit in silence, I start the conversation, "So, how's it going?"

Staring into this coffee, he says, "I'm sorry I haven't been around. The truth is... Erika and I are going through some shit. I was already working too much before because I couldn't handle what happened with Mom, and then... Never mind, that's not why I asked you to come... I'm sorry I haven't been there for you, and I'm sorry I haven't let you be there for me."

"I missed you, Donut Boy."

Nudging me away, he cracks a smile, as intended. "You gonna stop with that Donut Boy shit. Is my name still 12 in your phone?"

Smiling eagerly, I confirm, and he rolls his eyes.

Breakfast goes incredibly well, and I realize just how much I missed my brother. Trading half of our bagels, I'm reminded of the simpler times. "So, cemetery... Are we still going today? If you want to go, I will, it's just cold as fuck."

"On second thought, I don't think I'm ready to visit, but can I hold you to a raincheck?"

"More like I'm going to hold *you* to it," I smirk.

"I would like that, for real."

"Then you've got a deal."

He takes a bite of my bagel with avocado and asks, "So, what else is new with you? Why were you downtown last night?"

How did he know I was downtown? My question must be written on my face because he gives a sheepish smile and admits, "You forgot to stop sharing your location with me."

"Oh my God, you are the worst. You know that, right?"

"Yeah, yeah... Where were you?"

Using the hot chocolate to warm my hands, which are cold from the breeze pushing through the constant opening of the door, I ask, "You already know that answer, don't you?"

"It's possible."

"You completely abuse city resources, you know that, right?" The waitress chooses this moment to check in on us.

Raising his coffee cup for a refill, he thanks her, and she scurries away, blushing.

"Okay, so anything important I should know?"

Blowing to cool his coffee—because he drinks it black like a weirdo, instead of letting the cream cool it down—he stares at me like he's trying to decide how much I need to know.

"Come on, out with it. You don't get to decide what I know."

Finally, he starts to lay it out there. "He has a clean record, nothing to be concerned about."

"Okay, so why do you look like you swallowed a lemon?"

Thoughtfully, he stares at the ceiling. "You remember when Jenkins hit that kid riding his bike?"

"His drunk ass. Of course, I remember, what does that have to do with..." My words trail off as I get the meaning behind his expression. "That was Kendrick?"

He nods, and something clicks in my head. "Wait, but that was on the West side." My nose scrunched unintentionally.

"Not everyone grew up with the same kind of life we had."

"Why are you telling me this?"

"I learned my lesson after what happened with Nyshon. If he didn't want me to look him up, he wouldn't have given me his information, and with the picture of the plate you sent, I had everything I needed. I just thought you should know he seems like a nice guy."

My phone rings in my purse, "Sorry." I apologize and search around the bag stuffed with shit. Unsurprisingly, it's Kennedy.

"Bitch, you need to come to my house early so we can get you ready. I know you weren't supposed to be here for a few hours, but you should come now and tell me about what happened last night."

Spencer insists, "I've got the bill. Go ahead and have fun."

"Is that Spencer?" Kennedy yells into my ear. "Hey big brother!"

Chuckling, he says, "Wassup, Kennedy. Shanice is about to be on her way to you in a few minutes."

"Kay!" She says emphatically before hanging up.

"Good thing I made the decision on my own," I mumble. After giving Spencer a hug, I head out to my car. As I'm about to change gears, a text from him comes through with a link to an article headline. *Young man struck by intoxicated mailman donates half of his settlement to charity.* Spencer probably meant to show me this to reinforce the fact that Kendrick is a good man, but it only re-affirms what he said about performative care. He's been donating and caring for the community full-time, and I only participate around the holidays.

The entire time Kennedy is trying to hype me up to get ready, I'm numb. This afternoon, we're working at East Garfield Park at BuildBeyond. When I looked them up, I saw how much they're doing for the community, and I was excited, but now I can only question why I never thought to do this another time.

"So, how was it? Mind shattering? Soul repairing? His brother almost made me change my life, so I can only imagine."

"Girl, it was all that and more, but that doesn't mean it's going anywhere."

"Stop being ridiculous. You read way too many romance books to not realize exactly how this could end."

"Yeah, but it's not a book, it's real life. You don't meet people in a Christmas bar and then set off into the sunset."

She shakes her head. "No, you don't. But you do the work to become friends. *Check.* Evolve with chemistry. *Check.* Go on dates. *Check.* You're on the right track. Hell, sucking his soul out is like level six, so technically, you're ahead of the game."

"But who's to say he won't change his mind? Brandon was just like him before we got engaged."

"Sweetie, he's nothing like that lame muhfucka. You're wasting a chance at happiness because of someone who I wouldn't waste piss on if they were on fire."

"I know, I–"

"I'm. Not. Finished," She cuts into my practiced line of excuses. Crossing her arms, she continues her verbal assail. "Every damn day, people out here with the 'Fuck Cancer… RIP' posts, and you're squandering the second chance you got because of some dudes with mediocre dick. *Fuck* Brandon. *Fuck* Nyshon. May they get all of the karma they deserve in hell. Now, we're going to drop this subject, and let's finish getting you dressed so you can end this weekend with a bang."

Kennedy spins me in the mirror to inspect my appearance, and I'm still silent. What the hell do I say to any of what she said because there's really no rebuttal. She looks at me like I'm missing something, but I have no clue what it could be. She runs back into her room and comes back with these pretty present earrings.

"They're perfect, and you don't even have to return them."

"That's sweet of you, but you already know these will be back at your house the next time I see you."

"For someone who loves Christmas, you suck at receiving gifts, you know that, right?"

She places them into my ears and it's a cute look. My outfit isn't really anything special. My sweater dress is a long cable knit with a split at the thigh. Because it's still a work event, I'm trying to be presentable and pair it with some of the fleece leggings that keep me warm but look like regular tights.

I texted him to meet me here instead of at my place, so I'm not surprised when the doorbell rings at exactly three. Dancing, she sings like that viral sound going around, "He's heeeeere."

Today, he's dressed more down with a matching sweater that we didn't plan and dark jeans. Smiling, he says, "Two down, two more to go." Grabbing his hand, I wave bye to my bestie and wonder what's in store for us today. As my body warms from the contact, a flash of the other night plays in my mind, and the image of his face between my legs makes me almost trip. He quickly wraps his arms around my waist and squeezes my hips to pull me closer. *Not helping, Kendrick. Not helping at all.*

Chapter 23

Kendrick

"You're back again!" Brian says excitedly.

"You know I can't stay away from this place." Smiling, I shake his hand and re-introduce my girl. "I know you never forget a face, but this is—"

"Shanice," he says, finishing my sentence. "I forget plenty of faces, but this one isn't hard to remember." Brian places a kiss against her gloved hand and winks, but I push at his shoulder. He's clearly fucking with me, and it worked.

"Alright, alright. That's enough. Back away from my lady."

"Nice to see you again, Brian." Her voice is sultry without effort. Even on the coldest day, her smile brings sunshine and warmth to any situation. She's witty and smart as fuck, she's also inventive and caring. She's so much more than I feel like I deserve, but I can't fucking help the need to be close.

"Kendrick?" Her voice cuts through my fog of thoughts. "You ready to go in? I feel kinda weird just standing in the foyer here."

"Shit, I'm sorry, you're right. Let's get this going."

Her hand wraps around my forearm, bringing my attention back to her. "You sure you're okay?"

Doing my best to fake it, I smile. "Perfect, Bells. Come on, let's go teach those kids how to make some cookies."

Looking at my watch for the fourth time, I'm getting irritated, and the kids are getting restless. Waving Brian over, I ask, "Where's the baker? It's starting to get late." I feel Haverly's glare on my back, and I know she is questioning my decision to have the event here. She wanted to hire this big company to do this, and I insisted on staying within the community. I can't fuck this up because it will get back to Robert, and that's problems I don't need right now.

Whispering, he adds, "I haven't heard from her. I'm getting nervous, too, Kendrick. These kids are about to turn up in here."

From my side, Shanice asks, "Can I help?"

"Unless you're a baker, probably not."

Winking, she says, "Good thing I am then. Show me where everything is and what you want to make, and I can lead. There's no need to disappoint the kids."

"One second, Brian." Grabbing her hand, I guide her off to the side. "You don't have to do this. I didn't bring you here to make you responsible for this. It's my event, if anyone should be up there it's me."

She places her hand on my cheek and smiles, "I think the kids would like their cookies to be edible."

My mouth drops open, and her head falls back with laughter as her hand slides to my chest. My heart starts to beat rapidly, and I know she can feel it because she stares at the space where her hand rests before clasping them together and meeting my gaze. "It's fine, I promise. The kitchen is my playground. Let's go make these kids happy." Sashaying into the kitchen like her sway is a cloak of confidence, she stands shoulders back in the center, waiting for me to join her.

Brian and I stand beside her, and he starts talking. "Hey everyone, we're so sorry to keep you waiting here, but thanks to this woman here, we are going to get the event going. Today, we're going to make gingerbread cookies. The ingredients and recipe are on your station, but Ms. Shanice will lead us because I will straight burn these things without guidance." Laughter fills the room.

Speaking up, I add, "The kids have been waiting so patiently, so if the volunteers could split between the kids and introduce yourselves, it would be great. Chi Web Design is so thankful for you all coming and making these kid's evening. It's a gift to give back to our communities, and we're so thankful to have you as clients."

Everyone invited to this event is a client who works in the youth sector. Admittedly, I haven't completely understood the whole Holiday Fever idea for events because why do we need to catch up with clients once the project is done apparently three-quarters of those that attend appreciation events are listed on the referral forms when we get new clients. I guess there is a method to this madness. That doesn't mean I'll personally attend more of them, but I can stop deleting the emails when they come across my desk.

Tying an apron around her waist, she asks, "You ready?" The glint in her eyes is a little scary though, so I'm not actually sure I am, but here goes nothing.

"You've all done so amazing!" Shanice exclaims, walking around to see the cookies fresh out of the oven. Someone found this cute little Santa apron and watching her in it has me looking at her like a man starved. I want to see it on her with nothing else on. Sometimes, women get shy when it comes to me asking to watch, but if I can watch you please yourself, it makes it easier for me to learn how you like it. It's a cheat code, but it's also sexy as fuck.

"Okay, now you're going to pipe whatever designs you want. Be creative. There are no mistakes! If the volunteers could cut just a tiny snip off the top of the bags with color, I would appreciate it so much. For those of you who made circle cookies, we can add powdered sugar on top of those."

Thinking that I could help with that, I sliced open the bag of powdered sugar on the demonstration desk and put it into the circle thing she used to sift the flour. She's back in at the circle island with me and watching. When I go to crank the lever, nothing comes out, so I gently smack the side like she said.

"Let me help with that." She attempts to take the sifter from me, but like the idiot I am, I lift it on its side. Again, she tries to take it from me, but I'm not a little kid. "You shouldn't do that, Ken. Just give it to me."

The words she spoke, combined with the fact that she gave me a nickname, has me smacking the side of it a little too hard to prove I can handle this, but powdered sugar flies into my face. The room goes silent as people look at me like the idiot I am. I'm covered in powdered sugar on anything not covered by the apron, and though it blends in with my sweater a little bit, it's noticeable against my face and hair.

Her hands cover her mouth and nose, clearly holding in laughter. Her eyes twinkle with amusement. Brian returns to check on the progress and asks, "How in the world did you manage to do that?" Unable to take it any longer, I drop the sifter and laugh at myself. Everyone else joins in to laugh. When Shanice removes her hands, tears are pooling.

"It's not that damn funny."

"Oooh, he said damn." One of the kids in the back points at me, and Brian shakes his head.

Shit, I forgot about the kids, but Shanice is on it. "Mr. Kendrick has a potty mouth, and now he's going to get coal for Christmas."

She's still laughing, though, and I've had enough. Deciding that neither of us is leaving here clean, I crank the now-working sifter into her face. Her mouth drops as powdered sugar flies into her hair. One thing I know about black women and their hair— after living through multiple crises with my mom and sister—is that I am definitely going to pay for that.

Tilting her head, she nods and picks up a bag of frosting, but Haverly steps in before she can squeeze it. "Perhaps we should set a good example for the children," she says through gritted teeth. Louder, she continues, "It seems that both Mr. Kendrick and Ms. Shanice are going to get coal in their stockings this year. We appreciate all the time you've spent with us this evening. Once the cookies cool, you can feel free to box up what you made and take it home to your families. Kiddos, you'll have to check in with Mr. Brian on the way out. This was so much fun. Everyone give it up for Shanice. She saved the day!"

Applause starts slow. Then, it starts to grow as she curtsies. *She's so fucking adorable.*

"Come on Bells, let's clean up this mess." Looking around the room, watching everyone pack up their stations, I find Marshall wearing a proud smile. He gives me a thumbs-up before packing his container. It's one thing to mentor someone and be proud of them for their success, but him being proud of me... That just made my day.

Outside of the building, Shanice shakes her hair out as much as possible, then gives me a dirty look and hops up into my truck, ignoring my outstretched hand. "If my hair were straight, you would be paying to get it fixed."

All I can do is nod because she's right, and I would gladly hand the money over. I have more money than I know what to do with because of some investments I made when I was younger. It's not every day you get hit by a mailman while riding your bike, but if it happens... You apparently get a shit ton of money. It took me a long time to heal, but my parents were not playing games, and the city paid me five hundred thousand dollars. The newspapers said I donated half, but I'm no saint. I only donated twenty-five thousand. About half went into stocks, and the rest we lived on until my parents got into a better situation. The most extravagant thing I did was buy a small, half-rundown house. I still had to share a bedroom with Khalil, but it was ours, and it was warm.

"Where am I taking you? Your house or Kennedy's?"

Buckling her seatbelt, she answers, "Kennedy's. I *was* gonna go home, but it looks like I'm gonna need more help. Maybe I *will* have her straighten my hair. Hmm." In the mirror visor, she puckers her lips in thought.

"I like it like this." She raises a brow, and I quickly follow up with, "Not that it matters what I want or anything when it comes to *your* hair, but I like your curls."

She gives an approving nod, and I breathe a sigh of relief. *Thank fuck.* This woman sure knows how to challenge me.

For some reason, I let her play the holiday radio station on the way home. I'm happy she's in a better mood than when I picked her up because I realized today that I don't like sad Shanice. Seeing her light dimmed is a punch to the gut, and I'll do anything to change it. No matter how much I try to fight it, every day she works her way under my wall.

She must really be feeling the song because she starts dancing in her seat, singing out loud instead of humming. "Doesn't it feel like Christmas?"

Oh my God, she sounds horrible. "Who sings this song again?"

"Destiny's Child, duh."

"You might prolly wanna let them sing it."

"That's not nice! Santa heard you, just in case you forgot."

Mumbling, I respond, "I would be more concerned with him hearing you."

"You're an asshole, but I know, okay? Leave me and my horrible voice alone. This is my favorite Christmas song. Plus, the world wouldn't know what to do with me if I could sing." I got her to laugh, though, so my joke worked. She stopped singing and hummed again so I could tune out the fact that it was a holiday station.

Pulling up in front of Kennedy's house, I get out to help her down, not that she needs it, but chivalry and all that. "I'll see you tomorrow. Should I pick you up here?"

"Mmm hmm, I'll be ready at four. Thanks for letting me handle today."

"Woman, I should be the one thanking you. It would have tanked if you weren't at my side. I appreciate you. I'm going to walk these cookies over to my nieces down the block." Our kiss is gentle and leaves a promising feeling in my heart.

Normally, I would just walk because it's only about four houses away, but it's cold, and I see a spot directly in front. Like they sensed me coming, the front door slams against the stopper, and my nieces open before I can even ring the doorbell.

"Uncle Cheese!" Leah smiles and hugs me.

Luna cuts straight to the point, though. "What's in the box, Cheese Man?"

Holding the cookies high above their reach, I say, "Ugh, I thought we were done with Uncle Cheese?"

Making grabby hands and jumping while trying to pull my arms down, they say in unison, "Sorry, Uncle Kenny."

"How did my brother get in this house?" Kaliyah's voice booms from the kitchen doorway.

Ut-oh.

"Uh," Leah says while Luna mumbles, "Um."

Crossing her arms and standing at her full mama height, my sister tilts her head. "I'm waiting on an answer, ladies...5...4...3..." Each number gets louder until the point and decides to blame each other for opening the door.

"It was Leah!"

"It was Luna!"

"Kendrick Lavan Thompson, who opened the door for you?"

"Sis, I'm sorry. I honestly don't know what happened. I thought you opened the door." Ain't no way I'm snitching on my nieces. Yes, they shouldn't have opened the door, but they clearly saw me coming. Tears flow down their faces, and now I feel bad for even coming over.

She must notice at the same time I do because her eyes begin to water, but she closes them to take a second. "Sorry, I shouldn't have yelled at you, but you really can't open the door without permission, even if it's someone we know." She's terrified of losing them too, and that's something the kids don't understand, but I get it. After hugging them, she holds in all of her emotions until they're upstairs, then she crouches onto the couch and starts crying.

Sitting with her, I hold her close. "Sssh, it's okay. I got you, they're fine."

Pulling herself together, she sniffles, then asks, "What's in the box you gave them?"

Oh. "Um, I brought them some Christmas cookies from the work event I had today. Don't make a big deal out of it."

"Oh, but it is a big deal." Wiping her tears, she sits up, smiling. "Did you go to this event with Shanice by chance?"

Groaning, I push her away. "I'm leaving now. Don't let my girls eat all of those cookies. I don't want them to have a stomachache."

"Why do y'all think you can tell me what to do with me kids like they're yours? Did you go through all those hours of labor and push out those two big ass heads? No, pfft. Talking about my girls, boy, get out my house." She's laughing and in a better mood than a few minutes ago, so I'll take it. I literally only stopped by to drop off the cookies.

"Love you girls! Don't eat all those cookies." I yell up the stairs before heading to the door. "Love you too, sis."

"Yeah yeah." She tries to put on a front, but she loves me and loves when I annoy her. I'm not changing who I am because Christmas still sucks, but—and a small but—I think I can be less of an asshole about it.

Chapter 24

Shanice

"Okay, so red or gold dress?" Kennedy is standing, looking back and forth like she's the one who will be wearing them. Her question is rhetorical because I've tried to say I'll do the black dress she put back four times, but she keeps shushing me.

"Gold," I say, knowing she will pick the red.

"Okay, red it is!" She removes the gold dress from the door frame and puts it back into the garment hanger. But Jedi mind tricks always work when it comes to this. She thinks I don't have style, and it's eighty percent true. I have major decision paralysis when it comes to some things, and I'll fuck around and leave the store with nothing. My hips are wide as hell, but my booty doesn't match what you think it would. It's not tiny, but it's not as big as people think it's going to be. Mom picked this dress out, thinking I could totally wear it to a fancy Christmas party, but it's been sitting in my closet for two years.

Standing in lingerie while getting dressed for the last fake date with a man I've grown to like as way more than a friend. Is this still a fake date? I wonder if it's the right time to wear it. Mom thinks... thought... *I'm still not used to talking in past tense.* Mom *thought* it would be for something special. Kennedy helps me into the dress, and it fits like a glove.

"It's really pretty, but it's missing something." She takes a step back to look at me in the mirror. It's absolutely gorgeous, and when I hit a few dance moves, it moves with me and doesn't rip or bunch, so I'm agreeing that it's *the* dress. Picasso, I like it. Kennedy goes into her closet for a few minutes, but when she returns, she smiles like the Cheshire cat.

"What are you hiding?"

"Oh, nothing special. Just this..." From behind her back, she pulls out Mom's red faux fur half-coat with white trim around the top.

Gasping, I ask, "How did you get Mom's coat from Spencer?" I can't wait to put it on, but I also don't want to ruin it. Mom let my brother's wife wear this jacket but refused to take it back when she was done borrowing it, and she's had it ever since.

"Spencer brought it over yesterday, and your dad brought these."

Tears stream from my eyes when she opens the little jewelry box with the snowflake earrings he got her on their first wedding anniversary. "Why would he bring these?"

"I may or may not have told him you need a little Christmas spirit. I've noticed your spiral, boo. You can't let Pencil Dick or whatever extreme ass promise you made yourself get you down. Also, bitch don't mess up my hard work, stop crying." She dabs under my eyes with tissues and then follows with a bit of powder. I don't wear foundation, but this mascara will smear if I can't pull it together.

"Okay, I'm done for real. I don't know why I'm such a crybaby."

"It's cuz you need dick. You get dicked down enough, and everything doesn't make you cry."

Now that she's said something... "When was the last time *you* had sex? I haven't heard any of your escapades in a while."

"Psst. Pfft." She scoffs in multiple ways before turning her back to get more gold shimmer for the corner of my eyes. *She's hiding something.*

Narrowing my eyes, I lean close to her ear and ask, "What you hidin'?"

Caught off guard, she jumps to the side then nearly palms me in the face, but the doorbell rings.

"Something is wrong with you. You know that right?" She walks away, abandoning the glitter to look at the security monitor. "Oooh, it's yo boo."

"Girl, bye." He's drumming his hands against his pants while looking around nervously. *Glad to know it's not just me.* After a really quick dab of glitter, she pins a red bow in my hair to move my big ass mane out of my face a little bit, and we let him in.

Opening the door like a proud parent about to send her kid off to prom, she hums her approval of his charcoal suit. For some reason, my dumb ass thought he would have a red handkerchief or tie or *something* festive, but it's a regular suit. I look around for something that I can add to his lapel, just to give him a little something.

Like a mind reader, he shuts that idea down. "Don't even think about it."

I'm caught. Do I play stupid or call him out? "I have no clue what you're talking about. I can't find my phone."

Smirking, he says, "Check your hand."

Feeling like a complete idiot, I look down like I don't know it's in my hand.

"Come on, woman, I don't have time for your shenanigans today." Twisting his fingers with mine, he talks me through the plan. "One hour. I'm in. I'm mingling. I might even have one glass, but after that, I'm dippin', and I mean it, Shanice."

"Damn, so you gone leave me if I'm not ready to go?"

"I'll pay for your rideshare."

Rude. Shaking my head, I turn my gaze from him and look at the car we're about to get into for the first time. I notice the man with his hand on the doorknob, waiting to open it for us.

"Did you get a driver?" Aye, I can't even lie, that shit smooth.

He helps me first, then slides in next to me and places a kiss on my cheek when the door closes. "*Surprise!* I thought it would be a nice touch and a thank you for everything you've done."

"I didn't need all this, Kendrick. I appreciate it, but you didn't have to do this." Weird enough, I don't accept gifts well, but I love to give them.

Sitting back into his seat, he turns his gaze away then says, "I ain't *have* to do shit, you right about that. But you *deserve* it, so you *got* it, and I don't wanna hear not a bit of doubt about that from you."

Groaning, I realize he read me exactly.

"So, one hour?" He reiterates like the first time he told me wasn't clear.

"Or I'll take an Uber black home, and you'll pay for it, got it."

We try to hold it in, but we laugh and enjoy random conversations on the way to the event space.

On the outside, it's a standard-looking event building, but on the inside, it's decorated beautifully with three separate hallways, which hall is for which party. Each is decorated with different colors—the one with Chi Web Design is brown, red, and white. *That's an interesting choice.* Once I step inside, it becomes immediately apparent that the colors match. There are ceiling-height gingerbread houses. Finding an especially hilarious gingerbread man, I chuckle. *Oh my—*

"God, is that a giant gingerbread dabbing? Who the fuck chose the theme for this shit?" Kendrick voices my thoughts, albeit less amused.

"Is there a problem, Kendrick?" Marshall walks up with perfect timing, and Kendrick glares at him.

"Why the hell would you do this?"

"The guests happen to love this shit. So maybe take a look around before you start grumping."

Taking that advice myself, I notice how his coworkers are taking pictures in front of the giant gingerbread folks and pretending to live in the houses. It's clever as hell, but he won't admit that because then he would have to like something about Christmas.

Passing my coat to the coat check, Kendrick stares at me when the full dress is revealed.

"Damn, you look good."

Twisting side to side, I say, "Look, and it has pockets!"

"Why is that always the first thing y'all say when somebody compliments your dress? My sister does that shit too."

"Cuz that's all that matters. If you're really trying to impress a woman, compliment her dress having pockets. Most of the time, we know we look good, honestly; that's why we chose our outfits. But men noticing what, we think, are important details—that'll fuck 'em up." Winking, I add, "And that tip was free."

"Compliment the pockets after I say it makes your ass look juicy, got it."

"You're really annoying, you know that?" I still laugh, but yet, for someone who can be such a grump, he's charming as hell.

We rock back and forth to the music on the dance floor. I haven't brought it up, but we've definitely been here for over an hour.

At our table, he pulls out a chair for me and then whispers, "You know… I never asked if you were allergic to anything."

"I'm allergic to peanuts, and I don't eat pork."

"Damn, you got one of the big ones! I'm going to grab some food from the buffet for us. I'll be back with no pork or peanuts."

When he leaves, I search my clutch for my phone to text Kennedy. It's a lot packed into this tiny little bag.

Me: it's going well :)

Bestie: Good, now go have fun boo :)

I'm about to respond when I sense someone approaching me from behind.

"He seems to be having a lot of fun." Robert takes a seat next to me and watches Kendrick. "He's grown a lot in the last year, workwise, but that man is a tough nut to crack."

"That's for sure, but he also has an amazing heart under that shell. Even if he *pretends*, he doesn't. He's helping me with some personal projects at home, and I'm sure I don't need to tell you that man is excellent at what he does." Professional small talk, *I can do this*. Even if it's a little uncomfortable.

"Probably the best in the company, if I'm being honest, but let's keep that between us. He already has confidence the size of Jupiter." Unable to help it, I join his laughter.

Always one for perfect timing, Kendrick comes back to the table with a full spread. "Well, hello, Robert. I see you found my Shanice." The way he says *my Shanice* makes my heart thump against my rib cage.

"I was just stopping by to say hi. You've done a great job young man. The changes you made to the format of the events had the committee in a tizzy, but I think it's the best year of all. And this party..." Arms wide, he stands and gestures to the crowd, having a great time.

"And this party was all Marshall's doing," Kendrick admits. "As much as I would like to take credit for everything amazing, if it was up to me, we would be having a black and white affair."

"Well, I had better go find Marshall then and thank him for all his work then." Robert starts to walk away, but then he turns back around. "Kendrick, you impress me. Not just because of your work ethic—we all know you're the best—But because I just gave you the perfect opportunity to take credit for something you didn't do. We all know that the host isn't doing all of the work for these events, but you're the first one to admit it." Looking at me, he points to Kendrick and says, "He's a good man."

There's nothing I can say to refute that, so I smile and nod. Kendrick is speechless, and though he claims to be a man of few words, he usually has something to say. Scooting closer, I wrap an arm around him to hug him. He told me that what he misses most about his grandma is her hugs. I can't be her, but this seems like a hugging moment.

"Aw, look at y'all." We snap apart like we were caught doing something other than hugging by Marshall. "Ooh, food." He sits down at our table and waves one of the waiters over to bring a couple of glasses of champagne. Handing one to each of us, he raises his glass. "To a successful event and an amazing boss and mentor who just gave me the credit for the work I've done instead of taking it himself." Robert must have found him like he said he was going to. Our glasses clink together, and I smile at Kendrick.

We sit talking for what seems like an hour when Kendrick picks up what I know is definitely avocado hummus because I tried it already, and it is delicious, but he can't eat it. Panicking, I smack the cracker out of his hand, and it lands right on his white shirt. *Oh my God.*

"I'm so sorry, Kendrick." Closing his eyes, he clearly counts to ten before saying anything. Marshall's mouth is still wide open as if he can't believe I did that. "Let me–"

Raising his hand, he gets up to go to the bathroom to clean himself off. He shakes his head the whole way, and Marshall laughs as soon as he leaves the table. "Why'd you do that?"

"I don't know, I panicked."

"Panicked... about...?" Marshall prompts.

"Oh right, that dip had avocado in it."

"Shit." Without saying another word, he goes to the bathroom. Of course, someone should be helping him clean that off instead of cleaning it himself.

I ain't prayed in a while, but I'm definitely praying and walking right now. Praying while I walk, I also head to the bathroom to make sure he's okay. I stand outside the door and wait for them to exit.

When he walks out of the bathroom, I pounce.

"Jesus." He yelps when I grab his arm.

"Are you okay? I'm sorry, I should've just said that it had avocado in it, but I'm half fucking stupid. You already know this. Are you okay?"

Holding my chin, he says, "I'm fine. Marshall got to me in time to clean it off, but that was my sign that it's time to get out of here. We've definitely overstayed the hour I thought we would."

Shoulders slouching, I nod my agreement. As long as he's okay, I don't feel like an awful human.

"You want to go out to the little patio first? It's supposed to be heated. I can handle a few more minutes if we get out of there."

"I'd like that." Holding his arm, I walk alongside as we venture through the hall.

The frosty air is alarming when the doors open, but the scenery is mouth-dropping. Twinkle lights hang across poles above us and heaters line the space. After getting beyond the initial shock of temperature difference, it events out. The occasional breeze still raises chill bumps across my arms.

Without me having to mention I'm a little cold, his suit jacket is slid over my shoulders, but he keeps his scarf. "Thanks Ken."

"There you go giving me a nickname again, let me find out you actually like me."

Rolling my eyes, I respond, "I don't *not* like you. You've become a really good friend in the last few weeks." Friend is putting it lightly, but this is nearly the end of our deal and once we go back to only phone and text conversations, things might go stale.

Clasping his chest, his face distorts to a look of pain. "Friend-zoned, again. The pain."

Smacking his arm, I laugh, "Stupid." Changing the subject, I ask, "So, are you happy you came today?"

Thoughtfully, he rubs his beard. "You know... I am. This wasn't as bad as I thought it would be, but it's mainly because of the amazing company I have here."

"I am pretty amazing, you're right."

He stares at me for a long time, but no words come from him. Once the silence becomes uncomfortable, I ask, "I can't read you right now, Kendrick." Not that I can always read him, but usually, it's better than this. It can only mean one thing. He's holding something back *intentionally*.

Chapter 25

Kendrick

"I want to kiss you." Her breath hitches, and she looks at my lips as I move in. I get barely halfway to her when she jumps at me. Pulling me by the lapels, she leans me to sit on the bench. Using my thighs like her own personal seat, she puts that soft ass right on my dick. Rolling in circles, she moves her tongue with the same motion inside my mouth, and I'm getting hot as fuck with all these clothes on.

My hands roam across her thighs and find a slit at the knee I didn't notice before. Tickling against her skin, my hand slowly moves up her thigh until the tip of my finger slides under her panties and presses into her slit. She moans into my mouth as I move it in and out. Snow starts to fall on my head and face. When I open my eyes to take in the background, I remember being at a work event. I pull my lips away, setting her on the bench so I can compose myself. My elbows press against my knees as I heave in deep breaths. She's as still as a stone when she pushes beyond the glaze of lust.

Sliding my hands on my head, I apologize. "I'm so sorry. I can't believe I just—"

Smoothing her dress, she adjusts the bottom. "It wasn't just you. Honestly, the last few weeks were just so amazing, and I can't thank you enough for that."

Sitting up straight, I search her face for answers. "Why you talking like you're about to ghost me?"

"I'm not ghosting you."

"I've been thinking... What if what we need to get through the next few weeks is each other?"

"Kendrick!" Haverly interrupts our talk, but I definitely want to come back to this. "So happy to see you were able to make it. The decorations are absolutely amazing. You even danced out there for everyone. This was incredibly successful. I told you you would enjoy it! We really appreciate the touches that you made to how we run things here. If we're doing all that work to interact with our clients, we can add our local community to that."

Placing one hand on my bicep and wrapping the other to intertwine with my fingers, Shanice says, "I think you've stunned my man to silence here. If you wouldn't mind giving us a little time to work him through this, I would greatly appreciate it."

That was the nicest way to say back the fuck-up I've ever heard, though her tone made it impossible for her to hide her real feelings, no matter what her voice sounded like.

I lean my head onto her shoulder; my internal clock has been ringing the alarm for the last thirty minutes.

When my phone buzzes three times in a row, I remove it from my jacket pocket to find several text reminders from Mark.

Mark: Aye Sandz

Mark: don't forget I'm at the same venue

Mark: I'm in the hall right now with L.G.

Getting to my feet, I escort her around for the last time while also communicating the least amount possible with any of the drunken idiots in here. When we get our coats to leave,

I apologize. "My bad, Shanice. I just gotta say what's up to my frat. He's in the other room." Texting him back, I let him know I'm coming.

She jokes, "Oooh, you're a frat boy. How did I not know this?"

I laugh and shake my head, and then I spot Mark and L.G. across the hall and call out for them. "Yo!" I call across the foyer, but Shanice drops my hand when he turns to face us.

Mark's smile falters, falling to a scowl. I look back and forth to make sure I'm seeing what I think I'm seeing, and yeah, he's looking right at Shanice. His head whips to me, then back to her, then to me as anger flashes in his features. L.G. is as confused with this interaction as I am.

I turn back to find her frozen in place for short seconds before she pulls it together and sticks up her middle finger. Before walking away, she says, "Fuck you."

Mark tries to follow her, but I block his path. L.G. grabs his arm to pull him back, but he snatches away and then tries to walk around me.

"I ain't about to get in this shit," L.G. hoe ass says before walking away.

Mark shakes his head then says to me, "Look, this ain't got nothing to do with you, Kenny. I just need to talk to her for a minute."

"You don't need to do shit. I don't know what you thought was gonna happen when you saw her but leave her the hell alone. We frat and all, but when it comes to her, I'm not playing. Try me if you want to, I'll fuck you up, and that's on my grandmama."

Mark's jaw ticks, but he doesn't say anything as I stand, daring him to try it.

When he doesn't make a move, I turn to go and find Shanice. Walking away, I peer over my shoulder once more to add, "Maybe go home to your wife instead of trying to follow up behind *my* girl."

It doesn't take me long to catch up to Shanice. When I wrap my arms around her, she flinches and nearly knees me in the dick, but I block it. She's crying and shaking, and I want to go back inside and knock him the fuck out just because she's mad.

"You know Nyshon."

Confused, I say, "His name is *definitely* Mark, but yeah, I've known him since college."

"Well, the name I knew him by was Nyshon."

I spot the car and wave him over to us. When he pulls up, I don't make the driver get out. Instead, I open the door and help her in. Fire is flowing through my veins as I try to compose myself before entering the car on my side. The warmth in the vehicle chases away the child of the evening.

"Bells, I need you to tell me what's wrong. Did he hurt you?"

Scoffing, she responds, "*Did he hurt me*? No, I'm acting like this for no reason."

Whoa, I've never seen this attitude from her before. She warned me she had a problem catching an attitude when she went into defensive mode, but I ain't believe it— until now. "Yo, you can take that energy somewhere else because I'm here, and I'm not him. I know you've been through some shit, but you can reel that back. I'll rephrase, though... What he do?"

Groaning, she says, "Remember how I had an ex who was not exactly single? Yeah, that was him."

"Not exactly single? That man is full-blown married—with children. I'm not blaming you for what he did. I'm just saying... shit. I'm sorry. I wish that I could be surprised." Now I'm pissed. "He ain't shit and has never been shit. Matter fact, you want me to go back?" Hoping to make her laugh, I continue and quote a movie line, "You want me to go curse him out? Stomp him out in the street... whoop...that... ass?"

Snorting, she covers her mouth. "You're an idiot but thank you."

"I'm dead ass, though. I ain't no killer, but don't push me."

"Kendrick, *pleeease.*" Her laughter has finally surpassed her tears, but the ride continues in silence. Though she isn't speaking out loud, her thoughts are like energy waves, and by the time we reach her house, she's built a wall a mile high.

I grab the door handle to get out, but she holds me in place. "Please..."

"I was just gonna walk you to the door."

Leaning into my space, she kisses my cheek and whispers. "I need to be alone for a little bit."

"Can I walk you to the door?"

Smiling, she replies, "I never thought I would have to see him again because he lives out of state, but I'm happy you were there with me."

"Whatever you need, Bells."

"I need to be alone."

Nodding, I acquiesce and watch her leave the car ...*without* me.

Chapter 26

Shanice

Hold it together, Shanice. Hold it together.

My hands shake as I struggle to fit the key into my lock, but I refuse to break down out here. The winter chill bites against my exposed shoulders, and the weight of the evening has unshed tears threatening to spill over. When the door closes, my back presses against the door, I slide to the floor. Why the hell did he have to show up? Memories flash behind my eyes of the time we spent together. My stomach churns thinking of the wife he had at home on the weekends he would visit Chicago from Nevada.

The way he smiled at me was so warm and full of love. He treated me like I was his world when we were together, but he vowed to honor and respect one another. It was cruel. He's so fucking selfish. And then the fact that he dared to try to talk to me today? *What the hell was that even about?* That day in the kitchen, when everything went to shit, I stood there arms crossed, waiting for him to get off the phone, and he laughed at me. He fucking laughed in my face like me being angry was insane or unreasonable. He had the nerve to say, 'listening in *on conversations is only going to bring you heartbreak.*' Boy, *fuck you.* Finding out that his name isn't even Nyshon—I feel violated. It's one thing to lie about your relationship status, but lying about your identity. That's some next-level criminal bullshit.

The battered and bruised parts of me that have been ignored for the sake of moving on rise to the surface, and I scream, finally allowing myself to actually feel without pushing it down. I'm so angry; tears won't even come. Only the raw anger and the suffocating weight of my life's choices. Here I go again, catching feelings for a man who wouldn't measure up to Mom's tests either.

"What the hell am I even doing?" Rising to my feet in the darkness, I hang up Mom's jacket before sliding off the dress. Flicking the light switch, my home is illuminated, and I see the space for what it is, an illusion. I had this dream of re-creating the perfect Christmas. to honor Mom's legacy, but staring at my home, I realized how far I've spiraled. The perfect Christmas doesn't exist without her. There's no fucking reason that I was allowed to live and she wasn't. She was a better person than me. She took better care of herself. More people depended on her. It's not fucking fair! My body trembles as tears pour down my face, and I'm wheezing from only being able to take in shallow breaths.

"I'm sorry, Mom." The words come out strangled, and my voice cracks. "I wish it was me..."

The wave of sorrow within me shifts to determination. With trembling hands, I go to the fireplace and rip down the garland, the stockings, the snowflakes. Then I toss the pillows into a pile in the hallway, knocking things over on the table. Next comes the tinsel, the ornaments, the lights. Room by room, I rip everything down until it's barren, and the flood of emotions allows me to look around at the mess I've made. Decorations can't fill the void in my life without my mom in it. Nothing can replace her.

I thought doing all this Christmas stuff would make me feel closer to her, but I feel more alone than ever have. I've been stuffing distractions into a void that cannot be filled with men, Christmas decorations, or parties. Honoring Mom's legacy isn't about any of this stuff. Mom hummed carols while baking cookies and dances while organizing decorations. She loved and laughed and lived and shared that with us. It became special to me because she was special to me. Mom made Christmas feel magical because that's what she was—magical. All she asked me to do was leave that man, and I ignored her. I made her feel like she was crazy and that I knew better than she did because I was the one dating him. I've been overcompensating, but nothing cancels out the fact that I was too stubborn and fake happy because he wasn't beating my ass to realize that isn't a sign of a good relationship.

My phone buzzes in my purse, snapping me out of my thoughts. It rings three times before I finally get up to answer it.

"Why you not answering the phone?" Kennedy's voice is sharp, but concern is still laced in her irritation.

Defeated, I answer, "Hello to you too, Kennedy."

"Oh, I don't like that voice. You sound like somebody kicked your puppy."

"I don't have a puppy, Kennedy."

"Oh, *bitch* that's two times in a row you've said my name. I'm coming over."

"You don't have to–"

The telltale beep beep of the call disconnecting has me looking around the chaos. I guess I should put on some clothes. Stepping over the strewn decor, I go into my room and toss on a long t-shirt and shorts. Pulling my hair into a topknot, all I have the energy to do is wipe off this eye makeup. By the time I'm walking into the living room again, my front door is opening, and shock registers on her face.

"Oh, Shay." Words escape her as they do me. I didn't want her to pity me; this was pure rage and pain. Hot, uncontrollable tears finally make their way, and I collapse into her arms. She walks us over to the couch, and I cry and cry and cry until I fall asleep.

I don't know how much time has passed since Kennedy gently nudged me to wake.

"Hey boo. What happened tonight? Talk to me."

Everything pours out of me. She doesn't interrupt or tell me what I did wrong or what I could do better. She listens. When she opens her mouth to speak, my phone rings on the table. I check it to make sure it's not Spencer or Dad. It's Kendrick. Too drained to talk about this shit again I send his call to voicemail and text him instead. Is it rude? Probably, but I can't fathom talking on the phone right now.

> Me: Sorry, not feeling well right now, but I appreciate you being there for me tonight.

> Kendrick: Anything for you, Bells. It's never a problem.

> Kendrick: So, I'll see you at your family Christmas Eve party then?

I forgot he was supposed to help me with that. At this point, I don't even feel like I want to go myself. Kennedy is watching over my shoulder.

> Me: I'm not going to the party anymore

> Kendrick: baby, I thought you said you weren't ghosting me.

> Me: I'm not ghosting you, I just need a little time

His text bubble appears and disappears before his message comes through.

> Kendrick: I'll keep the evening open in case you change your mind.

I'm not changing my mind, though. *Not this time.* After what happened today, the only thing I need to plan is a call to my therapist. As I cradle a pillow, the emptiness settles, and for the first time ever, Christmas feels truly broken.

Chapter 27

Kendrick

Laying back on my couch, I stare blankly at the TV. I'm not sure what's on, but none of that matters right now. When I dropped Shanice off last night, she was shaking, and every protector bone in me wanted to pull her close and hold her until things felt better, but she didn't want me. When I first got this apartment, I thought it was sophisticated like this is how someone who has as much wealth as I do should live, but since Shanice told me that the whole thing is basically a beige crayon, I haven't looked at it the same since.

A knock on my door takes me out of my solo pity party. I forgot Marshall was coming over today. I haven't told him how the night ended when we left the event venue, but I still need to work on the bugs for this website. After everything she's been through, I don't want to be yet another person to let her down.

Stepping inside my apartment for the first time, Marshall pauses, sweeping a slow gaze across the space before wincing. "Why your spot so depressing? What you call this theme? 'I gave up and let the catalog decide?"

Rolling my eyes, I can't suppress the chuckle that bubbles out. "Whatever, not everybody out here tryna impress folks with decor, Marshall."

"Forget everyone. Impress yourself!" Marshall drops onto the couch, shaking his head. "Let's sit down and get this website finished so we can run a test because ain't no way you living like this. Let her fix this mess."

His bringing Shanice into this is a kick in the gut right now, but I'm trying to hold my frustration back. "So, what? You're saying even my apartment screams, I don't know myself?"

"See, even you agree." Marshall's smirk fades when I groan.

"Aight, let's say you're right. What you expect me to do? Bust down her door? She ain't answered my messages for days. Thanks to my idiot frat brother, she's been through enough. I refuse to be another one of her problems when she set a clear boundary. I'm not giving up on her. I'm giving her time to process."

Marshall clasps his hands together and leans onto his knees. "Alright, I could never have predicted what I'm about to say... But Kendrick, you're a fucking idiot. If you can't figure out what she needs from you, ask your sister what you should do."

My head snaps back toward him, "Fuck, you mean ask my sister? Why you say that like you know her personally?"

Snorting, Marshall says, "Boss, I'm literally paid to be all in your business. Plus, how did you forget that I went to school with your sister and that's how you got introduced to me? You thought you just charmed me into working here?"

Under my breath, I mumble, "I forgot about that." After he gets done laughing, we get to work.

In under an hour, we've picked up all of the bugs, and we're doing a clean run of the site now. I'm so excited about what this means for her business. My baby is so inventive and smart. Instead of asking questions about what people think they would like, she has people pick some pictures here. Rank photos there. When people are trying to get a certain look, they lie to themselves about what they want, but she makes it harder to do that. These calculations and algorithms are insane, and I want to know who built them. Clicking "process" feels so final, and I wait, knowing I won't see anything remotely like what I'm living in right now.

Marshall plops down onto the couch next to me with a bag of chips.

"You just gonna steal my snacks?"

Scoffing, Marshall throws a chip at me. "Please, you owe me at least a bag of chips."

Picking up the same chip, I throw it back at him. The computer beeps, and we look at the screen. It's actually buffering, which is a good step. The pictures start to pop up, and they're... blue—dark blue and white and pops of yellow. Tilting my head at the screen, I look at the options, and it's interesting. I don't know if I would have picked any of this, but I like it. No, I know I like it. I think I love it. Gazing around the room, I see the difference in how warm my place could feel versus what it looks like now. Testing the affiliate link, I watch as it links into a new browser and points to the correction item. Victory.

Marshall packs up to leave, saying, "Don't forget to call Kaliyah."

Mumbling under my breath, I say, "Yeah, sure. Right after this nap."

"Kenny..."

It's a voice I never thought I would hear again. "Kenny, open your eyes, baby."

If I do it, and she's not there, it'll break me. I'm terrified of the disappointment. I haven't seen Gran in my dreams for over a year.

"Alright, then baby. You'n wanna open your eyes, I can leave you here, son."

My lids fly open, and I stare into the eyes of the woman who raised me to be the man I am today. My parents taught me to be responsible and smart and never to keep reaching for my goals. But my grandma... Gran showed me how to love and be empathetic, and to desire.

In my dreams, she comes to me like she did when she was alive—rocking on her porch swing while humming some gospel hymn, smelling like lavender. "Is this it, Kendrick?"

"Is what it? Wait...am I dead?" Panicking, I feel around my body, feeling for a hole or an appendage missing.

"Son, is this what you want your life to look like?"

Shifting uncomfortably in my seat, I feel like a twelve-year-old under the microscope again. "This isn't how I planned my life."

Gran's laugh is full of disbelief. "Plans. You gave up on love because of one woman. A woman I told you not to try and marry, by the way."

"I didn't give up completely. I just don't wanna be blind-sighted or have my heart broken again."

"Did she break your heart, or are you just upset about starting over? I know it's been a while since you seen me, but I didn't think we would have to start from the top."

Her words hang in the air, heavy and unyielding. "Listen to me, baby, life is going to break your heart a hundred times over. But giving up? That's not in your blood. So, tell me, son—what are you really scared of? Come on and sit next to me for a minute." She pats the seat I normally occupy, and I lean onto her shoulder, enjoying the moment that can only last so long.

With each swing, a different memory plays before us. Me: opening Christmas presents as a young kid and the excitement well into adulthood.

"Now I know you miss me, boy, but don't be down there actin' like you lonely. That's your own damn fault. You ain't start being like this until that heifa Rose."

"Gran—"

"Don't Gran me! Don't let that woman ruin your joy."

"Did you ever ask Grandad for space?"

Laughing, she says, "Too many times to ask."

"Is that really what you wanted?"

"Now, why would I want space away from the man I loved? You and your lady friend need to heal. You both share this dumb idea that you need to grieve alone. What you need is support."

Beep. Beep. Beep. My alarm jolts me awake, but the message from my dream and Gran echo in my mind. It's racing, and I need to get out of this apartment. Lacing up my sneakers, I put on a heavy coat to go outside for a walk. The air is crisp, and the fresh snow creates a blinding brightness. My first Christmas with Grandma was so happy. I loved every part of the season. Grandad was a cynic, but he loved Grandma, and he made sure that even if he didn't enjoy something, he balanced making sure she was taken care of and supported. We ain't really have shit and were staying in shelters, but we were still helping donate our time to the community.

A flash of police lights whirring behind me caused me to stop and turn slowly. There's a cop smiling at me, waving me over to the patrol vehicle, but I don't know him.

Calling me my name, he says, "Kendrick, come here, man."

"Do I know you?"

"Spencer, remember?" I must have a confused look on his face because he rolls his eyes and says, "You probably know me by 'Donut Boy.'"

Snorting, I realize who he is and find myself willingly approaching a police car. "Guess I need to brush up on government names."

"You talked to my sister? She hasn't answered her phone in days, and I'm tempted to break into her house."

It makes me feel slightly better yet more concerned that I'm not the only one she pulled away from. How do I tell him what's happening when she doesn't want to talk about it? If he's concerned, maybe I can see what he knows first. "Do you know who Nyshon is?"

"What the fuck did he do?" His voice is gruff and full of venom.

Reluctantly, I fill him in with only the details of last night—the fallout with Shanice, her silence, the mess with Mark. Spencer listens quietly and intentionally. I can see him scribbling certain information I give him in a notepad.

"If I wasn't a cop, he would be buried. When it comes to my sister, though, you should talk to Kennedy. She lives by your sister, right? Just go stop by."

"Showing up at her best friend's house unannounced sounds like creeper activities to me. How you know my sister lives over there?"

Grinning, Spencer pulls out his phone. "You'll be surprised how much I know."

My phone buzzes with a text notification.

Unknown: This is Spencer.

Unknown: The other number is Kennedy.

Unknown: Edy, you talked to my sister?

Unknown: Stop calling me Edy

Unknown: What would the benefit be of answering that question?

Unknown: You've copied in the man, she's convinced herself she doesn't deserve when in fact they're both idiots????

Spencer looks up from his phone and says, "I know you see the same message I see."

*The group name has been changed to Ken^2 *siren emoji*

Deciding to be vulnerable, I ask for help. Before I forget, I change their names on my phone.

> Me: Very helpful, Ken2

Kennedy-shanice friend: Pfft, what makes you think I'm Ken2… I'm Ken 1

Kennedy-shanice friend: BUT Shanice is struggling right now. This entire thing sent her down a spiral, and she thinks she needs to withdraw to heal. She ripped down all the decorations.

Kennedy-shanice friend: It's a nightmare.

> Me: What can I do?

Kennedy-shanice friend: Get creative…

> Me: Again… Very helpful Ken2

Kennedy-shanice friend: I'm not here to help you, but if you want to help her, I'll think about it.

Spencer chuckles next to me as he reads her message.

"Whatever, man." I don't have any ideas, but her tearing her Christmas decorations makes my chest ache.

Back home, I feel more drained than ever. I slump onto the couch and scroll through funny videos until Spencer chimes in:

Spencer: Shanice likes grand gestures

Spencer: But you better mean it, or I'll fuck you up.

Kennedy-shanice friend: Ooooh I know!

A video call rings through, and I answer.

"Okay, I've got it." Kennedy is dancing and all excited. "I think Shay needs a pick me up. A Christmas miracle or something. She needs to know you value her. Watch her favorite movie—8 *Dates of Christmas*. It's constantly playing on the Romance Network."

"And what am I supposed to do with that?"

Shrugging, she says, "Well, that part isn't my problem, but I'm sure you'll think of something." After blowing a kiss, she hangs up. *Real helpful, Kennedy, real helpful.*

I can't believe I'm about to watch something on the Romance Network voluntarily; by myself at that. Even though I'm going to follow through, there's no way I'm getting through this without being high. Grabbing a few pre-rolls from my box, I light up and then press play. As the movie starts, the characters look familiar. It's cheesy as fuck, but it's not *completely* mid.

Like the nerd I am, I'm sitting here taking notes, trying to figure out why Kennedy wants me to watch it. Then again, they're also high notes, so I'm sure I'll laugh at this in the morning. Ole dude basically convinced shorty to date him by making sure she understood he could accept her for who she was. It's hard not to roll my eyes at the predictable plot and corny ass dialogue.

By the end of the movie, I'm two blunts down with a half-eaten bowl of popcorn and three pages full of notes. Even if it's lame, I get why he did what he did. He hates Christmas for different reasons than I do, but there's value in having someone around who isn't as much of a cynic. There's also balance, especially when embarrassment is my reason. By the time the credits roll, I finally understood what Kennedy wanted me to see and opened the group chat.

> Me: I think I've got it.

> Kennedy-shanice friend: it's about damn time.

> Spencer: let's hear it

For the next forty-five minutes, I text back and forth with her people. It will take a lot to pull this off, but I will do it. I'm doing all eight dates in one day. *Lord help me.*

Chapter 28

Shanice

"Knock, knock!" I'm flipping through design magazines when Jenna, Ted's assistant, peeks her head into my office.

"Shanice! The shuttle is about to pick us up for the holiday party. You coming or driving by yourself?"

Not answering the whole question I respond, "I'm not taking the shuttle. You have fun." *I'm going home early instead.*

She gets halfway out of the door but stutters in her path before turning around. "Wait, are you *not* coming? That sounded a lot like 'have fun without me.'"

Trying not to be annoyed because she didn't do anything wrong, I say, "I'm passing, Jenna. Christmas just... I'm passing. I'm just really busy right now." It's not a lie. With the best smile I can plaster on, I follow up with, "You have fun, though."

Thankfully, Jenna doesn't press for answers. She lingers only a few more seconds before nodding and retreating. Exhaling deeply, I curl my hands on the edge of my desk, attempting to shake it off. The truth is, I'm not fine. Every mention of Christmas, every decoration, every carol playing softly in the background of this season feels like another reminder of what's missing. *Mom.* Getting back to work, I let the barrage of tasks from the first official client distract me.

My phone rings on my desk. Nobody has called me in a few days, so this is a nice surprise. It's Spencer, thank God. "Hey, Spencer."

"Who are you, and what have you done with my sister?"

I can't help laughing. I haven't just called him Spencer in years, but now I'm wondering if it actually bothers him that I make jokes about his job. "I just decided to try something different." Hesitant, I ask, "Does it bother you that I make fun of you being a cop?"

"Nah, it doesn't actually bother me. When I first joined, it stung a little bit, but now it's just a running joke. I know you still love and trust me. Don't have your little friend over there calling me Donut Boy, though."

Snorting, I say, "You don't have to worry about that."

"What did you do, Shanice?"

"Hey, I didn't do anything. I just need a little break."

"Why?"

"Why what?" I didn't know I needed to explain.

"Why do you need a break?"

Here I was thinking that he was going to be the one that didn't ask me a lot of questions.

"Would you rather me ask why you've been skipping out on the Christmas countdown?"

Ooh, he went there. I'll take question number one for five hundred, Alex. "I don't want to fall down the same trap as I did before. I'm listening to Mom this time."

The line goes silent, and I take it off my ear to make sure that he doesn't hang up. "Hello?"

"I don't know what—What did Mom tell you, Shay?"

"She said not to trust someone who doesn't like holidays. It was the same with Brandon and Nysh—Mark. I'm trying to listen this time."

Groaning, he says, "You only half listened to what she said, but color me shocked. That applies to Nyshon because he's a cheating, lying asshole. I'm not even going to refer to that other motherfucker because he's dead if I ever see him again. What she was trying to tell you is to pay attention to the clues. If he's barely around and claims to hate holidays, it's because he has a family to spend it with. That's what she said, and I know it because she told me the same shit. I listened, and I'm *still* on the brink of divorce, Shanice."

Fuck. I know he said stuff was rocky between them, but I didn't know it was that bad.

"Look, I'm not telling you to make you feel bad. I'm telling you so you get your head out of your ass. Even if you decide to date him, Kendrick might not be the person you marry, but you might miss out on the person who is supposed to be your person if you don't let that go."

Like he senses my rebuttal, he says, "Yes, I know Kennedy is your person, but unless y'all are gonna change your minds and start fuckin' you need a partner."

"I *could* always go back to dating women."

"You're so fucking intentionally difficult you make me want to tase you."

"Ah, there's the cop coming through."

His bellow of laughter takes me off guard because he normally ignores my mentions.

"I love you, Spencer."

"Love you too, sis. Dad and I are coming over tonight to watch Polar Express. You better have some cookies."

"Yeah, yeah." Hanging up, I look at the clock and realize I really need to get home to clean up. I guess I'm making cookies too.

Dad and Spencer show up at my doorstep a few hours later with popcorn, drinks, and pizza. After hanging his coat up, Dad asks, "What um—what happened in here?"

Avoiding their gaze, I take the drinks to the kitchen. "I cleaned up. Y'all ready to watch the movie?"

They take cautious steps forward and wrap me in a hug before I can protest. Judging by the fracturing in my heart, I needed it.

"Niecy, listen to me," Dad says in a soft but steady voice. "Your mom loved Christmas, but more than that, she loved you. She loved us all. That's what mattered to her."

"But she—"

"No buts." Spencer chimes in, his arms heavy around my shoulders. "You're not alone in this, Shay. You've got us. And if keeping these traditions alive feels too heavy, we'll carry them for you. Together. I'm sorry if you felt like you were alone in this."

Dad pulls away to brush the tears I didn't notice had fallen. "Tonight, we're going to watch The Polar Express, and then tomorrow, we are going to keep on with the Countdown to Christmas and go to breakfast at the normal spot, just like we used to. Do it for me."

Despite the weight of grief pressing against my chest, I agree, "I can do breakfast." We sit and laugh and remember Mom's favorite parts. I feel better knowing I don't have to do this alone. We've spent so much time in our grief separately that we didn't pay attention to how much we actually needed each other.

Standing in front of my closet the next morning, I can't figure out what to wear. It's cold as hell outside, but I don't want to look like Randy from A Christmas Story, either.

Huffing, I hop onto my bed and call Kennedy.

"Bitch, it's eight am. Why you calling me?"

Whining I say, "Kennedy, I need your heeeelp."

"Who the fuck are you, the Looney Tunes? What you need my help with?"

"I can't find an outfit."

"You got a date or something?"

"No, but I can't figure out what I want to wear to breakfast."

"You woke me up at eight am because you need help finding an outfit for breakfast? Don't make me unalive you."

"Well, I'm going with Dad and Spencer, and I'm trying to pull off the not-sad look."

"Wait, what's today?"

"It's the twenty-third. What does that have to do with anything?"

"Shit, my bad. Let me wake up for real. Hold on." The video call comes through, and I accept, but she's brushing her teeth, which is normal until I see a foot.

"Aye, who over there?"

Turning the camera, she says, "Mind your business. Now, show me what you're thinkin'."

Deciding I'll press her for details later, I go to my closet and pick out three sweaters, but she vetoes all of them.

Rubbing her chin, she says, "None of this is working. Hmm. Oh, I've got it! Have you washed those fleece leggings that look like skin yet? Wear those with the black corduroy dress and your red turtleneck that matches those red boots we got on clearance."

Ooh, that's a good idea, actually. "Okay, I love that."

"Great, she loves it. Now come back to bed." Hold the fuck on, I know that voice.

"Kenne—"

She hangs up before I can finish her name, but a smile spreads as I realize she decided to run Khalil back after all. Then I get sad because I miss Kendrick. Despite me asking for space, he texts me random things to make me laugh, but nothing that requires a real response.

Noticing the time, I hurry to get dressed and grab my keys. After my talk with Dad and Spencer today, I'm tempted to turn on the holiday station, but I'm sure I will get plenty of that in the restaurant. The drive is only about fifteen minutes out of the city. Mom loved this place because of how they make it look like Santa's Village every winter, and when I pull up to the front, my eyes mist from the memories. Last year, we didn't come at all, but this year... it's the first year coming with her, and that burns.

Looking in the mirror, I say, "No tears, hoe. It's breakfast. You can do this." The cold air slaps me in the face when I exit my car. Dad's car is here, but Spencer's isn't. Usually, Dad is the one who's late. Entering the shop, the smell of cinnamon and roasted coffee beans greets me before the host gets to.

"Welcome! Happy ho-ho-holidays. Table for one?" She's cute and bubbly, reciting her little Christmas lines with a cheery smile. I miss being young and unaware of the real responsibilities of adulthood.

"Shanice!" My name is called from the back booth. Dad stands, waving at me, looking happier than I would expect him to be, but he did get here early. The booths are high backs, so it's near impossible to see who is in it, but he's in our normal spot.

"That's my dad. Thanks!" I walk around tables full of patrons enjoying food I can't wait to inhale. My mouth waters just thinking about it. Reaching the back booth, I realize that something—or someone—is different.

My breath catches in my throat before I'm able to form words. "What are you doing here, Kendrick?"

"Shanice!" Dad scolds me like I know better, but really. *What is he doing here?*

Kendrick stands and waits for me to take a seat. I stare warily because this has slight stalker vibes. Pointing between them, I ask before sitting down, "Uh, so how'd this happen?"

Spencer replies, "I actually met Kendrick at the park the other day. When I saw him walk in alone, I said, " Hey, he should sit with us. So, he's here."

My brows furrow with confusion. "You're acting very strange."

"Yes, I am." He admits.

"Sit, *we do not turn people away during Christmas*," Dad says with finality, just like the dad in 8 Dates of Christmas. I guess I'm having a seat.

I feel the need to sit and be silent after that scolding, so that's what I do. Somehow, Kendrick fits into their dynamic. Spencer tells a story about his kids, and I can't help but smile and eventually laugh. The food is delicious, as usual, and their cinnamon chai coffee is probably my favorite thing on the menu. Holding my cup close like a precious gem, Kendrick takes another chance to talk to me.

When Dad and Spencer go to the bathroom like girls in the club, he leans close. "I know. I'm probably the last person you expected to see here. I'm sorry if this ruined your countdown plans."

Searching his eyes for sincerity, I find it easily, and a flicker of warmth spreads across my chest. "You didn't ruin anything." And that's the truth. This breakfast—while unexpected— has been the highlight of my week. Maybe Spencer was right. Not that I'm going to admit that again, but it's nice having Kendrick around.

Chapter 29

Kendrick

I didn't think this all the way through. Well, that's not true, I planned today down to the minute, but if she says no— fuck I hope she doesn't say no. My palms are sticky as we leave the restaurant. Her dad snuck off to pay the bill, which she assures is the norm for him, but I put cash on the table for a tip.

Walking toward the door behind her, I can see the sleigh. Parked in front of the restaurant is a horse-drawn sleigh, its polished wood glinting in the winter sunlight. Mitchell's old rich ass ain't have nothing better to do. He uses this "sleigh" in the town Christmas parade, so I'm lucky to have that connection. Gasping, she runs to the window, face to the glass like a kid and a toy store.

"Dad, do you see that?" The reverence in her voice makes me feel like I'm off to a good start.

"The horses have antlers! Oh my God, this is so cute."

Hands shaking, I try to talk, but my voice cracks. I clear my throat and start over. "Would you like to go for a ride?"

Spinning to face me, her mouth is open like she can't believe it's a possibility. "Shut up, are you serious??"

Taking her hand within mine, I nod at Mitchell, dressed in full Santa costume. She looks back and forth between us, then to Steve, her dad, and then to Spencer, and punches me in the arm.

"Ow, what the hell, Shanice?"

"This *was* a setup. I can't punch Dad because he's old—"

"Hey!"

"And Spencer's a cop."

"I will definitely arrest you."

"And I don't know him," she says, pointing to Mitchell Santa. "But you..." She emphasizes her point by punching me again. "You can get punched."

"That's domestic abuse, and I can definitely arrest you for that," Spencer says, deadpanned.

She attempts to hide her incredibly obvious middle fingers behind her hand, but Steve chuckles. "Was Kennedy in on this too? Never mind, of course, she was."

She's spiraling. Maybe she's not used to anyone doing something nice for her just because she's her, but we're changing that today and for a lot longer if things go the way I'm hoping.

A wave of nerves crashes over me, and I wonder if this is the right plan. *I wish Gran were here to affirm me.* With that thought, a warm pressure squeezes against my bicep, and I spin around, thinking someone grabbed me. Shanice is looking around as well, but no one's there.

"You okay, Kendrick?"

Exhaling all of the doubt, I reach into my memory to pluck out the movie line. "*The moment I saw you, it felt like my heart wouldn't be whole until I knew your name. Now I'm just hoping you'll agree to spend the day with me.*" She gasps and pokes her lip out. It's cheesy as fuck, but I hope it works.

Softly, she says my name. "Kendrick." When she walks away and paces in the corner, I think I'm shit outta luck, but when she turns around, she's smiling and nodding.

"You'll go with me?" Her head is bobbling nonstop like she can't find the words.

"Thank fuck," Spencer mumbles.

"Gimme your keys, honey. I'll make sure your car gets home."

After giving her dad her car keys, she takes about twenty pictures with Santa and the horse-deers that jingle from bells around their necks with every sway of the wind. This is about us both healing. I can't let an evil person ruin my joy and steal a great woman from me. I can't let her think she has to be alone or that she isn't worthy.

Helping her into the sleigh, I slide the thick fur blanket over our laps. The part of me who lusts after she envisions all of the things I can do under this blanket—but this ain't that. It's about creating a nice memory for her to remember the holiday with a positive note. To help her remember what she's missing and honor her and her mom's favorite movie, I need to do this right. In a way, it's what she did for me. If I end up being able to call her mine officially when this is all over—that's a dream come true.

"I can't believe you did this! How'd you know that movie line?"

"A birdie told me to watch it." Leaning forward into this seatback pocket, I grab the two canisters. "So, I tried my hand at this one recipe, but it sucked ass, so instead, I made Gran's RumChata dark hot chocolate. If you don't like it, we can stop and get some along the way."

"Along the way where?"

"Do you want me to ruin the day, or do you want to experience it real time?"

"Hmm. Real time!"

That's how she was going to get it anyway, so I'm happy she decided to go with the flow. The sleigh takes us through the heart of the neighborhood. Admittedly, this would look cooler at night, but I'll have to repeat this later for the full experience of the glowing lights and inflatable snowmen. People smile and wave as we pass. Kids point and jump like it's their turn next, and I feel a little bit like a jerk because I didn't consider that part.

Finally taking a sip, I find myself randomly overwhelmed by grief. Notes of the creamy vanilla I got in the Dominican brings out the velvety texture of the hot chocolate. Gran made this every year to start off the season. It's been three years since I've had it, and I squeeze my eyes shut to stop the tears from leaking out. I'm just happy to have someone to share it with.

The warmth of the alcohol isn't enough to push away the chill flowing to my bones. We planned out a twenty-five-minute route since we are in a time crunch, but I wish we cut it a little shorter since a lot of the events are outside.

Trying to text inconspicuously, I text Khalil.

> Me: Khalil, can you grab some extra hats, gloves and scarfs for us? The temp is colder than I thought it would be.

> Khalil: meet you where?

> Me: uh… Millennium

> Khalil: bet

I slide my phone away and wrap an arm around her. She snuggles deeper into my side, sips the homemade drink, and then asks, "How long is the ride?"

"Getting cold?"

"Yeah, a little bit, but this is still so amazing. I never thought I would be able to do this."

"If I didn't better understand the last person you dated, I would question what type of person you like."

"You're such an ass."

Rubbing her arms, I laugh, "That's true sometimes, but I'm also the type of man to do this for you, just so you have no doubt you're special."

"That's not from the movie."

"Nah, that's just for you." I kiss her forehead. When I look up, we're already in front of the dance center. I try to be inconspicuous when I check my watch as Mitchell pulls over.

"I ho-ho-hoped you like this ride, young people!"

Her face wrinkles up with confusion when she looks at me. "Are we walking to your car?"

Christmas music starts to play from the studio on her side. She sits straight up when the curtains open, and a full set of the Nutcracker is on display. We don't have time for a full ballet, but for the right price, the studio was willing to let us watch their dress rehearsal for the parade. I may have asked for something a little special at the end to match what happened in the movie.

Shanice sways side to side, smiling during the performance. The climax begins, and three kids scurry to the front with boards. They flip them around, and they read Merry Christmas Shanice, but the words are upside-down. Tilting her head, she gasps and covers her mouth. An adult pops into view and the small crowd that has gathered smiles as they're flipped right-side up.

Turning her chin to face me, I lean close to whisper in her ear. "*I don't care what it is, snowboarding, baking cookies, or watching The Nutcracker with you, I'm all in.*"

Her forehead drops to my shoulder as it becomes clearer what's happening.

Once the curtains close, the sleigh starts again and heads to our next destination. About a block away is a gift-wrapping store. I had a bunch of gifts delivered, and we'll slow down just a little bit in the warmth and wrap presents.

Shanice is walking into the store giddily beside me.

The store clerk looks outside and perks up, instantly realizing who we are. The people helping me have all become way more invested than I thought.

"Mr. Kendrick, Ms. Shanice." The store owner says warmly, gesturing toward a pile of neatly stacked boxes inside. "I'm

Anna, and I'll get you going today. Here are all the toys you ordered. Once you're done wrapping, we'll take them to the shelter, just like you requested. The tree is already set up."

Shanice turns to me, her eyes wide. "You did all this, personally?"

"I figured you wouldn't mind helping me. Gran told me I'm shit at making bows."

Laughing, she says, "I can definitely help with that."

Anna shows us a few different techniques to wrap the gifts, along with adding bows and tying ribbons. This is definitely more complicated than I thought. I am admittedly a fancy bag buyer because I am horrible at wrapping, but the dude in the movie picked it up quickly, so how bad could it be?

Side by side, we wrap gifts—well, I *try* to wrap gifts—but both of the ladies are scolding me for tucking skills I apparently don't have.

"If you do that again, I'm going to ban you from wrapping any more presents."

"Hey! What'd I do?" I thought I was doing a good job. Anna is silent during this exchange, but I see the corner of her lip twitch before she sucks them between her teeth.

"You're a well-intentioned sweetheart, but the kids should feel like Santa and his elves prepared their gifts for them. Yours look like something the kids could have done. No offense," Shanice says.

"Did you know that if you say something mean and then add, no offense, it does nothing to take it away?"

Anna snorts, then covers her mouth. "You all are adorable, I'll let you two sort this out." When she scurries to do something else, I look around and spot a bunch of bags and gift paper.

"Does Santa bring gift bags?"

"Of course, why?"

"Okay, so I'm actually really good at that." I grab some bags and gift paper and head to the counter. "Can I add these to my bill?" It's a dumb question because what's she going to say—No?

Once the additional supplies are paid for, I set them on a table and look around for the odd key-shaped toys that would be more difficult. I'm thankfully able to find a dozen. Though Shanice is tucking her little fingers away, she keeps sneaking peeks at me to figure out what's going to happen. I'm confident with this ability, though. I match the gifts up to the bag by size. The trick is making sure that the gift can barely fit into the bag and wrapping the gift with paper, too. I roll a stuffed animal between two sheets, then gently add it to the bag. After folding and tucking a few sheets that match, I step back and marvel at my masterpiece.

"Looks like you found yourself a job, Ken. That looks so good."

I thought I would be saying this line while I was wrapping gifts like he did, but we're freestyling now. "*I'm a man of many talents, and I'll try anything if it means I get to spend more time with you.*"

Pinching the bridge of her nose, she sniffles. Her words are forced as she says, "You're not going to make me cry. You're not but thank you."

I kiss her forehead again and get back to it. For the next hour, we sit wrapping and stacking presents into a huge bin. When I planned this day, I made it about her not becoming me. I tried to decorate after Gran passed, but I ended up ripping everything to shred in my rage from her death and Rose's betrayal. It took me until the gingerbread decorating and everyone saying they missed seeing me around that I abandoned them. Sure, some people only come during the holidays, but as an all the time face, it's a letdown when I don't show up for two months every year.

Apparently, Shanice isn't the only one that needed to heal.

Chapter 30

Shanice

I can't believe he's doing all of this for me. Kendrick being at breakfast was a shock in itself, so I didn't put together the accidental meeting connection when Dad asked him to stay. The sleigh ride was a dream, but when it got to the kids performing, I just about lost it inside. Though I smile gently, my walls are shattering brick by brick. The fourth date was wrapping gifts.

He's not copying the movie exactly. He's making it his own, and that's even better. We all love a good billionaire romance, but Kendrick is going about this a whole different way, and that's what makes it so much more special. I know exactly what happens next, but he's so big into giving back to the community that I doubt he spent the money for a private car on a holiday train. *Don't anticipate, Shanice. Participate.*

Our walk from the gift-wrapping store to the train station doesn't take long because it's only a block away. With how cold it is, I'm happy. Arm in arm, we walk in silence, though I can sense his gaze randomly sneaking a glance. My only goal today is to try to hold it all in.

This is the best way to honor Mom, by living and taking advantage of the second chance she didn't get. My heart fractures thinking about her, and a fog of cold air builds around me when I exhale those emotions. Kendrick opens the door for me to enter the tunnel so we can walk over to the tracks.

"Oh, thank fuck." He says, and I agree with those sentiments. "It's definitely colder than the forecast said it was going to be, so I apologize for all of the outdoor stuff. I called the bat-line, so hopefully, the rest shouldn't be so bad."

"It's okay, this is perfect, even though my toes are basically icicles."

We laugh and walk toward the platform. The monitor says the next train is in fifteen minutes and that gives us plenty of time to stay warm.

"So, uh. Are you uh—Are you liking this so far?" His body is rigid like he's waiting for a blow, but he's going to get no complaints from me.

"I could never have guessed anyone would do something like this for me."

His shoulders drop, relief evident, and although this might not be the best time, I need to know what happened to make him this anxious. "Why are you so nervous like I wouldn't enjoy this?"

He mumbles, "This conversation would be better if I was high." Grabbing my hand, he pulls me over to a bench off in the corner. "You're not the only one with an ex that fucked you up. Three weeks ago, I would have told anyone that I was over her, but meeting you made it apparent that I wasn't."

"Ouch."

"Wait, no. That's not what I meant. Rose was what I thought I wanted, but all I was to her was a pocketbook. If I had done this for her, she would have complained it wasn't grand enough. It wasn't showy enough. I think that I was just so in love with the idea of love because of the examples in my life that I was willfully ignoring signs that should have smacked some sense into me."

That sounds painfully familiar.

"In the middle of a giant Christmas Eve party, I proposed to Rose in front of all those people. She said no."

"No."

"Yuppp. The worst part was hearing her girlfriend in the background laughing and then walking off together without a single care that they just ripped out my heart. The icing on the fucked-up cake is this happened a few weeks after Gran died, too.

Clearing my throat, I try to find the words to say. I was not expecting him to say she was cheating with a woman. "I'm sorry that happened to you and that she was such a shitty person. You shoulda' known she wasn't shit by her name. There was plenty of room left on that board for Jack."

Snorting, he says, "See, that right there. I think God sent you to challenge me because you're everything I need but also everything that terrifies me. When I got that first email from you, I smiled all day. Because I didn't want you to get in trouble for me accidentally responding to the wrong one, I had Marshall print them out for me. I have all of 'em in a folder, and I know that's weird as hell, but I've had a little crush on you for damn near the last three months. Meeting you in person is the most kismet thing I've ever experienced in my life."

"I don't know what to say to that. It's probably the sweetest thing that's ever been said to me."

Standing, he extends a hand to help me up. "That was my explanation for my hesitation. I'm not expecting you to say anything, *except* you'll take this gummy with me."

"You want me to take an edible before we're about to get on a train full of kids?"

"It's gonna take like thirty, forty minutes to kick in. Nothing's gonna happen."

"Famous last words, but, yeah, let's do it." One gummy isn't going to do much for me except make me giggly and calm my nerves, but I guess that'll help when I have to be around screaming kids and parents who don't actually want to parent their children.

When we hit the platform, I'm floored because the train is so much more amazing than I could have imagined. There's a candy cane vinyl wrap around the front with garland and tinsel. Inside, the ceiling has colorful lights and hanging ornaments. Kendrick's eyes are bouncing back and forth at each monstrosity of a decoration. I love that he's doing this for me, but no. "We don't have to do this one."

"I'm that easy to read, huh?"

"You're a bat signal away from a panic attack."

Laughing, he hangs his arm over my shoulder. "Come on, Bells. It'll be fine. *What's a little Christmas magic without mayhem?*"

There he goes again, quoting lines from the movie and making me all emotional and bubbly inside. I've imagined that I was the main character in that movie way more times than I care to admit and to be living it. Well, I don't feel like I deserve it. We sit on the top rail so we can people-watch, just in time for Jingle Bells to blast over the speakers. Kids sing along and bounce in their seats. The attendants walk down the aisles passing out hot chocolate and cookies when one of the kids trips one of the servers, and she falls—hard. The car goes silent when she doesn't get right back up. Kids start wailing and parents freak out. At the next station, we have an emergency stop for paramedics. A conductor helps her to her feet eventually, but she's got a major concussion. The conductors are discussing what to do because they're missing a server, and super save a hoe himself stands and starts walking down the steps.

"Gentlemen, I apologize for the intrusion, but I overheard what you said, and I can help if you need a hand." I know this motherfucker isn't over there really about to try and help like this edible ain't about to kick in. He waves to me, and I grump my way down. "They only need us to clear the garbage. Easy peasy."

Twenty minutes later, we are both a *little* high, smiling and singing Christmas songs that playing with the kids and parents. I even performed part of the *Hot Chocolate* song when it came on. I adore Polar Express. Now, the train is cleared, and we've been gently reminded to have a seat at least twice. The tunnel darkens, and we sit back to watch the lights.

"You ready?"

I'm not sure what I have to be ready for, but I join him to walk up the ramp. I haven't been to Millennium Station in a while. The ceiling tiles still aren't fixed, and that seating section could use new chairs, but the smell of popcorn, coffee, and fresh bread lingers in the air.

"It's a little crowded here, huh?" He asks, looking around.

"Yeah, I don't remember it being this busy, but it's the holidays, so people might be shopping."

"True, true."

Just then, a hum starts to build. It starts out low but grows quickly until a bell dings. *Wait... I know that beat.* Near the front, a group is gathered, and through their speakers, 8 *Days of Christmas* plays over the speakers. When I'm ready to hum along with the words, the group starts to sing. It's a choir of rich voices, and I'm so happy I'm here to experience this. I know downtown there are street performers, but what's the likelihood...

Kendrick spins me in a circle, and I see the dancers approaching from the tunnels. Date number five was Christmas caroling, and he paired it with a flash mob. I *didn't know those were even a thing anymore!* I don't know the dance moves, but I sway and shake with the beat while humming, well aware I can't sing.

Kendrick starts to two-step with me within the swath of people, harmonizing with his sexy ass baritone. Hell, he could have caroled to me himself. Jumping at him, my lips meet his for the first time today. Wrapping his arms around my waist, he pulls me closer and closer. Cheers sound around us, and his eyes are glazed with desire when he pulls back.

My skin tingles when his fingers brush over the side of my face to move a stray curl.

Bringing his face close to my ear, he smooths my hair away from my ear and then licks along the edge of it. "You lucky we in public, woman."

His name comes out breathy. "Kendrick."

Pulling back to grab my cheeks, he says, "What I'm supposed to say is *your voice makes my heart skip a beat*, but I heard you sing the other day, so that would be a lie."

Shoving him away playfully, I walk off. "Lick my asshole, Kendrick."

"When beautiful?"

Well, that'll do it. The butterflies fluttering beg me to tell him to skip to the good part where he throws me over his shoulders and licks me like his favorite flavor of ice cream. He interlocks his hands with mine, and I look down and marvel at how well they fit together.

"Why don't you wear gloves? It's like twenty degrees outside."

"I'm a manly man. Ruggedness and all that, I don't need gloves."

"You lose them, don't you?"

From the side of us, a familiar voice says, "He takes them off and places them on whatever surface he can find and then doesn't try to look for them, is the truth. That's why I brought some clips for my poor big brudder."

"Fuck off, Khalil. Thanks for bringing them down."

Hmmm. I wonder if Kendrick knows where Khalil was before this, but he doesn't stick around long enough for an interrogation.

When I turn to Kendrick, his head is tilted sideways, staring after his brother. I'll let him handle that later. I still gotta talk to Kennedy about it.

"What's next?" I ask.

"Put these hand warmers in your gloves, baby. He brought you a thicker hat and scarf, too."

"Oooh, I'm baby now?" You can see my molars with how hard I'm smiling.

"You been baby, I think *we* just now realizing it."

"Now you out here running lines on me." I shake my head. "Where are we going now?"

"Chriskindl Market. It's not too far of a walk."

Cuddling into his side, I match his pace as we walk in silence. Honestly, it's too cold to think in this weather. I might get a brain freeze.

The large log nutcrackers come into view, and we snake through the roped entrance into Chicago's annual pop-up Santa's Village. Wooden stalls glow with twinkle lights across the rooftops as the scent of freshly roasted nuts, spiced wine, and hot chocolate almost distracts from the fact that it's crowded *as hell*.

My eyes catch onto a little glass angel that reminds me of this glass ornament Mom used to have. He kisses my forehead, and I turn to find him smiling down at me. Our lips meet for a gentle kiss until someone bumps into us and breaks the trance.

The line for the mulled wine is long, and I'm half second-guessing if I'm going to get it.

"Hey, I gotta use the bathroom really quick. I'll be back, Bells. Do you mind staying in line?"

"Um, yeah. No problem."

"You sure? I can hold it."

Pushing him off, I smile. "Ken, go to the bathroom."

Smiling brightly, he jogs off, twisting side to side to weave through the swath of bodies. He's swallowed by the crowd, and I keep up with the snail's pace through the line.

Moments later, gloves glide along my waist from the back. Kissing the top of my head, Kendrick announces, "I'm back. Did I miss anything?"

"Oh yeah." Leaning to look back at him, I say, "You only missed Dasher and Dancer doing their pre-flight warmups."

"Did you sit and think of that the whole time I was gone?" He gets back just in time to order and grabs up some souvenir nutcracker mugs.

"Nope! I just came up with it right now."

Before I take a sip, he slides a candy cane into the glass.

"Oh, you're just full of little surprises, huh?"

"*I figured you could use a little extra magic this year.*"

My heart pounds as I take in everything that he's done for me. We've known each other for less time than any relationship I've ever been in, but he's more thoughtful than any of them. Sure, he might not pass the mom test, but he didn't fail it either. Burying my face into his chest, my emotions get the best of me. "It's perfect."

Hand in hand, we continue walking along, drinking our wine and picking out random little gifts. Each moment of this day has unraveled my carefully built walls. Only I can decide to push beyond the fear, the loneliness and grief, but I think I'm ready to try–with Kendrick. Maybe that's what mom meant by saying Christmas to be important to us together. Christmas isn't about the decorations or the traditions themselves, but the people you surround yourself with and the things we do together. Maybe I didn't have to be alone. *Not anymore.*

Chapter 31

Kendrick

A notification from the driver comes not a minute too soon. It's cold as fuck out here, and we need a break from the chill before the final stop of the night. My palms are clammy, and my nerves are shot, but I hope I pull this shit off. Grabbing her hand, I speed walk to the corner where the car is waiting.

"Whoa, we in a rush?" she asks, trying to keep up.

"Not really, I just figured more time in the car would be warmer."

Gasping, she starts walking fast, "You had me at 'inside.'"

I open the door to the Escalade, and she hops in, melting into the heated vehicle with a sigh that's half relief and half exhaustion. Climbing in after her, I notice a tray of food laid out with a note from Marshall. *I know y'all forgot food. You're welcome.*

"I could kiss him," Shanice says, already dipping her chicken tenders into the mild sauce.

A spike of jealousy stirs, and I say, "Yeah, aight. Keep playing." My nose wrinkles as I watch her commit a crime. "You're eating them wrong."

"We listen, and we don't judge!"

"Huh?"

"Never mind." She mumbles, shaking her head and taking another bite.

Both of us succumb to a food coma during the hour-long drive from downtown to the Botanical Gardens, but I'm woken up when the driver says, "We're here, sir."

Gran loved this place. It was the first place we went during the year. The trees, lit with warm white lights, welcome us in the darkness. It's been a long day, and I think we both needed this nap. We are not twenty-one anymore.

Shanice is asleep on my lap, with her arm curled around my thigh. Her lashes flutter when I move her hair from her face, but she doesn't attempt to get up.

"Wake up, Bells."

She groans and burrows deeper into me. "But I don't wanna."

I know today has been a long day, and maybe I should cancel this.

"Bells, do you wanna do home? We don't have to do the last one if you're not feeling up to it."

Her eyes finally open, foggy but curious. "I'm tired." Finally looking around, she shoots to a seated position, putting her face against the glass. "Are we at the LightScape? Kendrick, did you bring me to the LightScape?!"

"Would that be a good thing?"

Instead of answering, she grabs my face, slides onto my lap, and presses her lips to mine. It's soft, deep, and so full of gratitude it almost knocks me off balance. My hands find her waist, grounding her as I kiss her back. The driver picks the perfect time to remind us we aren't alone.

Clearing his throat, he asks, "Are we staying or leaving?"

Freezing in place, she stares at me with wide eyes. Since someone has to answer the driver, I confirm, "We're staying. It's supposed to be about an hour if you want to leave."

"I'll wait here, just in case," The driver chuckles. "My wife and I came here last year around the same time, and let's just say we got through the path quick."

Laughing, we listen to the words he didn't say and layer ourselves for the cold.

Sliding on the sweatpants I asked Marshall to send, she mumbles, "Finally, someone who thinks."

Each exhibit feels like stepping into a new world, and I snap pictures, getting permanent memories of her reactions. Her eyes sparkle as we walk through tunnels of lit candy canes, and she dances as we watch light shows that match the beats of the music. At the waterfall of glistening lights, she sits on the bench like a mermaid. Lights bobble on the water in another exhibit, and I take a deep breath to get ready. Approaching the large willow tree with dangling lights, I notice the employee holding the small sign with my initials on it.

"Is it over?" She pouts like we haven't been traversing for damn near a mile down the path, but I grab her head and approach the man.

"Kendrick Thompson, that's me." He stares between us like I could be wrong.

Crossing her arms, Shanice says, "Your sign only has initials. How would he know the name if it wasn't him?"

If ever there's a problem, a black woman is going to fix it. Is it her job? *Hell nah.* Is she going to do it anyway? Let's enter the last minute as exhibit A.

"Sorry, sir. Ma'am. This way, of course. I apologize, but there have been four people who have tried to guess the name of the VIP attendee, and you just happened to be the first ones who were right." Turning quickly, he fumbles, opening the black rope to allow us back and weaving us through a dimly lit path away from the main trail.

The closer we get, the more nervous I get. Entering a secluded area, she looks at me with a very confused expression, but little by little, the space around us illuminates. Twinkling fairy lights cover the tree trunk and every individual branch. While it's not the fanciest thing I could have imagined, there is a tiny little sprig of mistletoe. I roll my eyes, but it will have to do.

Holding her hands within mine, I start. "You've clearly figured out what's happening today, and baby, I'm so thankful for your patience because doing this in one day has made this a long fucking day, and I'm old as hell."

She laughs with mist forming in her eyes.

Lowering my forehead to hers, I say, "Bells, you've helped me see beyond grief and anger. You've helped open a side of me that I thought would never come back to life. I knew from the first time you emailed me and said "same," instead of reporting me, you were loyal. From the moment I laid eyes on you, your aura captivated me. When your lips touched mine for the first time, I fiend for another taste. When our bodies connected, I was ruined."

Using her gloves, she wipes away the tears streaming down her face. "Kendrick..."

"Almost done, baby. After meeting you, I wondered if I was ever in love before because there's never been anyone to make me feel how you make me feel. And I've never cared about anyone the way I care about you. I think about you all day. I see funny things and want to send them to you. I bring your name up in a conversation that has absolutely nothing to do with you. I think I'm one trip away from falling in love with you, and I don't want to let go of what we have growing between us."

Sniffling, she says, "I think I may already have."

My lips connect with hers, and our bodies heat from our connection as the winter cold is warmed by our desires. Pressing one more gentle kiss to her lips, I pull back and take out my phone. "One more picture, Bells."

In a teasing tone, she says, "You said that ten pictures ago." She still stands close to me as I frame us perfectly. Since I'm using the selfie side, she finally notices the mistletoe hanging from the branch. When she looks up and smiles, I snap the picture as I stare at her face, just like the movie cover.

Looking at the picture, she gasps, "You really thought this through, didn't you?"

"I wanted to make sure that you knew that even if I'm not the biggest fan of consumerism during the holiday season, I can understand how your connection to your mom is brighter when you're celebrating. I don't want you to lose that. I think we both needed to be reminded this year that Christmas isn't about gifts, decorations, packages, or events. I think we needed to realize it doesn't come from a store, but from the memories within us that mean so much more."

Leaning away from me, she asks, "Did you just rip off the Grinch speech from the end of the movie?"

Unable to hold a straight face, I burst into laughter. She joins me, shaking her head. It's getting colder, so it's time to wrap this up.

"But for real, he was right about it, and I *want you to meet me under this mistletoe every year. And every year, I want you to remember that I'll love you just as much as the last time we kissed underneath this same tree. I wanna wake up to you every morning and fall asleep next to you–*"

She jumps into my arms to kiss me, and we fall to the ground. With every kiss, she says another word. "You. Are. So. Special. And. I'll. Be. Here. Every. Year." Grabbing the back of her neck, I kiss her until light flecks of water start to smack me in the face. Blinking, I look to the sky and find snow falling, making this the most picturesque evening.

The next morning, we wake with our limbs intertwined under the sheets at my apartment. It's been a long time since I had a woman in my bed, and we didn't have sex. It's not that we didn't want to, but we passed clean out after our shower. Even now, my legs are heavy as hell, and I don't wanna move from this bed.

Kissing her nose, I say, "Mornin' Bells."

Stretching, she yawns, "Hey, Ken. I could sleep for like three days."

"Same, baby."

Climbing her fingers up my chest, she sighs. "You hog the sheets, just in case you didn't know."

Mmm hmm, I know for a fact she sleeps like a wild animal, but I'll let her have it. "Sure, baby. I'm about to take a shower. You wanna join me?"

"I took a shower before I went to sleep, didn't I?"

"Mmm hmm."

"Then no, I'm going back to sleep."

"Okay baby. Happy Christmas Eve." I kiss her forehead and try to walk away but she grabs my arm, cheesing.

"Did you just wish me a Happy Christmas Eve?"

"Yeah, why?"

Smiling all hard, she says, "You love me."

With a gentle kiss on her lips, I wink and respond, "Maybe I do."

Chapter 32

Shanice

When Kendrick gets into the shower, I have a silent, solo celebration.

"*Maybe I do.*" He completely loves me.

My phone rings with a call from Dad.

"Hey Niecy, you had a good time yesterday?"

"You have no clue. It was amazing, and I don't know if I'll ever be able to repay him."

"Well, baby. When people do things for you out of love, it's not a debt. I don't know if he's realized it yet, but that man loves you."

Rolling onto my side, I say, "Love you, Dad."

"Love you too. Niecy. That's not why I'm calling, though."

Dread pours over me, and I pray it's nothing bad. Hesitantly, I ask, "What's wrong?"

"Aunt Rie canceled the Christmas Eve party for tonight. I know you normally look forward to it, so I figured I would give you a call."

This is a saving grace more than a disappointment. "It's okay, Dad. Thanks for letting me know." Not that I don't want to talk about memories of Mom, but her sister is dramatic as fuck and will make everything about her.

"Happy Christmas Eve!"

"Happy Christmas Eve, Babygirl."

When he hangs up, I stare at the ceiling, unsure of what the day will bring now. In a manic rage, I ripped down all of my decorations, and I barely felt like buying presents this year. I spent so much time focusing on things that don't matter that I neglected the things that do—rather, the people that do.

Wrapped in a towel, Kendrick comes back into his room, brushing his teeth. Oh, I need to do that. I'm not sad, but he must have noticed the change in my energy.

"What's wrong?"

"Nothing really, my family's Christmas party is canceled. More time for naked activities." Wiggling my eyebrows, I attempt to move his towel and look, but he swats my hand away.

"Hands off the merchandise, woman."

Pouting, I make my feelings known. "Boo!"

"Oh, later on, I'm going to make you ride my face until your legs don't work no more. But first, I'm going to ask one more favor."

"What's up, baby?"

"I'm baby now?!" Kendrick exclaims with a wide smile. "It looks like we might be able to squeeze in a little time after all."

I laugh and scoot back to the headboard, faking like I'm running away. "Focus, Kendrick. What do you need?"

"First, Ima need some of that pussy, then I need you to go to my family Christmas Eve party with me."

"You were going to go to my family's party when your family has one? Why?"

"Shanice, I been about you. I need you to realize that. Plus, I haven't been in a long time. It just felt incomplete. Plus, the last time I was at the family party, I got embarrassed."

How could he be embarrassed at a Christmas—oooh. That's when she turned him down. If I ever see shorty, I'm beating her ass because that's wild. In front of his whole family, too.

Peeling my clothes off, I crawl toward him and say, "Yes to both."

His towel is tented from his obvious desire. Biting his bottom lip, he says, "You're saying yes to both?"

"Mmm hmm. Now come over here before I handle this myself."

"Baby don't tempt me with a good time. I'll watch you play with that pussy anytime, but the party starts in a few hours, and I still need to take you home to get dressed. Roll over and crawl backward."

By now, I know he means what he's saying. On all fours, I crawl backward down his bed and watch as his hand glides up and down his dick. Deciding to be disobedient, I turn and suck the head into my mouth.

"You don't listen for shit, huh?" He grabs the top of my head, and I swallow him down.

He allows me about thirty seconds before he pulls back and spins me around, then shoves his face between my legs.

I moan, "*Fuck me*," when he adds his fingers.

Smacking down hard on my cheeks with his other hand, he promises, "I'm about to."

From behind, he licks one last stroke, then rubs his tip against my clit until I'm coming. As promised, afterward, he inserts himself and yanks me against him. I rock back to meet his strokes until he pushes down on my back, so my chest is pressed against the bed. He lifts one of his legs onto the frame of the bed. Power stroke after power stroke hits me deep in all of the right places. Before long, we're both spent and sated.

"Maybe I changed my mind," Kendrick says, speaking between inhales. "Maybe we should stay here and do this all day."

As amazing as that sounds, I think he needs to go be with his family, but I'll be right at his side.

Standing to get into the shower, I say, "Good try. Now you gotta shower again because you're sweating. First one in gets to drive." I use the advantage I got from being on my wobbly legs first to run into the shower.

"Gimme the keys, Kendrick." He's holding onto the keys to Shantel, but I won. Maybe it's not fair and square, but who cares about that?

Dangling them in front of me, he says, "Don't be turning corners all hard in Roxie."

"I renamed her Shantel, remember?"

Shaking his head, he crosses his arms, "I didn't agree to that shit. Call her Roxie, or you can't drive her."

Damn, that's wild. "Okay, okay. Roxie"

Giving in, he tosses me the keys, and I hop into the sexy beast of a pickup truck. Rubbing the leather steering wheel, I say, "I promise I'll be gentle."

He raises an eyebrow. "You better be. She's not as forgiving as I am."

I have so much fun driving and talking to Kendrick. It feels natural. I like this. I *love* this.

"The house is up there on the left."

As I'm parking his truck, I ask, "Is it too late for me to turn around? I'm nervous."

"What you nervous about?"

"I've never met family before."

"Excuse me?" His eyes widen, full of disbelief.

"What? I haven't. Even though I was engaged, I didn't meet his family and high school doesn't count."

He blinks hard like he's unsure of what to say to that. "Well, my family is crazy and loud, but they're fun, and they'll love you. Come on, woman."

His parents' home is truly a home. Pictures fill the mantel. Homemade ornaments adorn the giant tree in the foyer. It looks loved in here. The party is in full swing, and the hum of conversation and laughter quiet at the sight of Kendrick.

A beautiful black woman with streaks of silver in her hair and big brown eyes runs up. "Kendrick, you came!"

Kissing her cheek, gives her a side hug and says, "Hey Mama, this is my girl, Shanice. Bells, this is my mama. Over there waving with the crusty beard is my pops. Actually, can y'all just introduce yourselves?"

I can't wait to text Kennedy with the update because yeah, their daddy is fine as fuck too, but he doesn't get up to greet me or Kendrick. Clearly there is a reason he doesn't talk about his dad.

"I'll give her the tour." A woman who must still be in her twenties locks her arm within mine. "Sorry about my brother, he has no couth. I'm Kaliyah, but I'm sure you've heard all about me. These are my girls, Luna and Leah. You already know the twin." Whispering, she says, "And nobody else really matters."

"Uncle Cheese!" The girls exclaim together.

I have heard a lot about Kaliyah, well, to a lot of details, but he talks about her the most. "Nice to meet you. Why do they call him Uncle Cheese?"

"Let's just say, if bro consumes dairy, run away."

His insistence on oat milk is so much more hilarious now. Apparently, that's enough of the introductions because Kendrick pulls me away toward the fireplace.

Kendrick leads the prayer before we eat. His hand rests on my thigh for most of the meal, but I can't tell if it's because he needs support or if he thinks that I do. His dad talks and makes jokes with just about everyone except him.

When we play games, Kaliyah tags me to be her teammate, but Khalil argues that he met me first, so he should get first dibs. They're a lot of fun. Though I'm distracted from the pain of the past, I notice Kendrick isolates himself, so I excuse myself to join him.

I wrap my arms around his waist and hug his back. "Hey, you okay?"

Turning to face me, he says, "Okay is relative, but I'm doing alright." Resting his chin on my head, he gets quiet for a beat while rubbing circles with his thumb. "My parents are great parents, and they've been a great example of a happy marriage, but after Gran died, I took things really hard, and we drifted apart. Sometimes, they made me feel like I was overexaggerating about my grief, so I distanced myself. How could I be taking the loss harder than her own son, ya know? But now I realize why it hit me so hard."

From the doorway, his father steps through, "Because your grandmother was more than a grandmother to you. She was your beacon of light when things went bad. She was your confidante when things went wrong, and I was jealous because my mom loved you more than she loved me."

Kendrick is squeezing me for support as his father joins our private moment.

Kendrick shakes his head and says, "She didn't love me more than you."

"Look, Son, the version of your grandmother that you got was not the mother I had. Now don't get me wrong, I still loved her with my entire being, but I couldn't say the same for her." He steps closer to place a hand on Kendrick's shoulder. "I'm sorry if I invalidated your feelings. That wasn't my intention, but now that I'm hearing it, I understand why you pulled away. I'm sorry, Kendrick. I miss my son." Letting him go for a moment, I allow them to embrace. They share whispers back and forth, and I notice Kendrick's body shaking.

When his dad pulls out of the hug, he nods to me and mouths. "Thank you."

Once Kendrick levels out, we take a final lap of the party. When the cousins head out to take their "walk," I'm stopped by Kaliyah.

"Gimme your number," she demands.

Rattling off the digits, I wait for a text to come from her and save her contact.

By the time we get back to Kendrick's apartment, I'm exhausted. The magic of the day has officially worn off, and now I just need a good night's rest. Kendrick got restless in the middle of the night, and when I woke, he was still missing, but low music hums in the background.

"Is that Christmas music?" I mumble through the fogginess of sleep. The smell of bacon rouses me from the bed. After brushing my teeth, I put on one of his shirts. When I walk into the living room, there's a huge tree—fully decorated. Tears pool in my eyes when I notice him dancing in the kitchen while making breakfast.

He turns, wearing a bright smile.

"Merry Christmas, Bells."

"You did all this while I was sleeping?"

Shrugging like it's no big deal, he says, "I can't imagine celebrating our first Christmas together without a tree."

"I wish you would realize how special you are, Kendrick."

"Same, baby. Go sit down, and I'll bring you breakfast."

Apparently, breakfast is the only meal he can cook, but it's delicious without being fancy. I fill up on everything he's made, and we lay on the couch and watch *How the Grinch Stole Christmas*.

When I come back from a bathroom break, he's holding a small, wrapped gift. "Is that for me?"

He nods, and I sit down and carefully unwrap the gift to find the glass ornament that I was admiring at the Christkindl Market. My heart swells with appreciation. "How'd you get it?"

"I took a detour during my bathroom break. Do you like it?"

"No, I love it."

His lips brush gently against mine before he says, "And I love you."

My heart races with a mixture of joy and vulnerability. A soft and uncontrollable smile spreads across my face as everything I want crystallizes in those three words.

My stomach twists in nervous knots and my throat feels tight as the weight of speaking my feelings swirls a mixture of excitement and fear within me. I can't compare him to any man I've loved in the past because what I feel for him is so much stronger than loving him. I'm in love with him, and that realization brings certainty and strength to how I feel. "I love you too, Kendrick."

Our mouths connect as we seal our truths to each other, but my phone starts buzzing incessantly.

"What the hell?" He grumbles while pulling away so I can take a look.

Unsure of what it could be, I open my phone to see over twenty text messages firing in rapid succession.

Kaliyah has added Shanice to the Forever Heauxs chat

> Kaliyah: Everybody say hi to Shanice.

> Kaliyah: Merry Christmas

> Unknown: Not yo ass out here barely popping in the thread, then adding new people

> Unknown: Who is Shanice?

> Unknown: Girl, I ain't heard from you in a month

> Unknown: Really Kaliyah?

The messages continue on and on until I turn off the thread alerts. Kendrick laughs and slides my phone across the table. "Kaliyah done added you to her friends' group chat. You for real a part of the family now."

In this moment, under the glow of the Christmas tree and the warmth of the moment, everything feels exactly as it should be.

Kendrick pulls me back to his chest and says, "Merry Christmas, Shanice."

I snuggle into his side and ask, "You remember when you hated Christmas?

With a hearty laugh, he pulls me closer to him and says, "Yup, but that was before I had you."

Epilogue

18 Months Later
Kendrick

"Are we really doing this?" Shanice asks like we haven't discussed it ninety million times.

"Bells. Breathe, baby. Everything is going to be okay."

"But we're both quitting our jobs. Are we sure we're ready for that?"

In the last eighteen months, I've learned that Shanice needs to think things through three times. Her website has taken off with so much more success than either of us could have imagined. Initially, I thought she harbored a lot of self-doubt, but in time, we figured out she just has really bad anxiety.

Not going to lie, that shit was hard as fuck. It took her two months to agree when we decided to move in with each other. When I asked her to marry me, she was so anxious about me changing my mind that I flew us to Vegas, and we got married the same day.

"Let's walk through it."

Holding her hands, I ask, "How much do we need in savings for a year as a cushion?"

"Sixty to survive, eighty to thrive."

"What did you earn on your website last year, baby?"

Mumbling, she says, "Two hundred."

"Yup, two hundred thousand, which gives us multiple years of cushion, right?"

"But Robert just offered you, partner. That's huge, Kendrick!"

"Yeah, it's a big deal for someone who wants it, but I—me...Kendrick—I don't want it, baby. I wouldn't be able to do any of the community projects and giving back means more to me than anything else." I've opened up to Shanice about how I grew up and why it means so much to me to do what I can. For most of these people, all it takes is one bad decision or a layoff. If I have to give that up to move to a higher level, that higher level isn't for me.

"What if I fail?"

Now we're getting to the root of the issue.

"Let's put it out there. You could. You could fail, *but* if you never try, you don't know if you could succeed. We're up all day every weekend, adding new links. If we focus on our dreams, we can dedicate twice as much time but also live twice as much."

Her eyes bounce around, and I can tell her puzzler is puzzling.

"Mrs. Thompson, we're doing this, and it's going to be great. You are talented. And as we found out, there's a lot of fucking introverts who don't wanna do all this peopling shit. Now we can open the market, so other people can see the benefits too."

Blowing out a deep breath, she leans her forehead on my chest. "I love you, Kendrick."

I cradle her head against my chest, pressing a kiss to her temple. "I love you more, Bells. Always."

Her arms snake around my waist as she sighs, her body relaxing against mine the way she does when she is sure about her choice. I know this isn't just about quitting her job or stepping into the unknown. This is about trust. Trust in herself, me, and the life we're building together.

"I just don't want to screw this up," she murmurs, her voice muffled against my shirt.

I tilt her chin up so she's looking at me. "Listen to me. You're not going to screw this up. And even if things don't go exactly as planned, we'll figure it out. Together. That's the whole point of this, right? We're a team, baby. You don't have to do it all on your own anymore."

"You always know what to say to get me out of my head."

"Yeah, well, I've had eighteen months of practice."

She smacks my chest lightly, but the tension in her face is fading. "Fine," she says, finally confident. "We're doing this. No more second-guessing."

"That's my girl."

"Okay, *Mr. Thompson*. What's the first thing we're going to do as two newly *self-employed* entrepreneurs?"

Grinning, I gesture toward the couch, where her laptop is already open. "We're going to finish adding those new links to the site, then celebrate with some eggnog cookies—your specialty. And after that..." I trail off, winking.

Shanice rolls her eyes but can't hide her smile. "You're ridiculous."

"You love it."

"I do," she admits, her voice soft. "I really do."

As she sits down to pull up the website, I watch her with pride swelling in my chest. This woman—my wife—has no idea just how unstoppable she is. And together? We're going to make something incredible.

The future doesn't feel so scary anymore. It feels like ours.

The End.

Maybe :)

Acknowledgments

Phew. It's done.

I wrote this long beautiful note for the first book that I wrote because I thought it was going to be the first one that was released but here we are. I wrote a whole second book, wiyald. There were so many moments where I almost gave up. This book exists because of persistence, love, hope, and the unwavering belief of so many people. Most times I didn't think I could do it myself.

To my husband—Dee. Your patience during this entire process was TESTED and I thank you for giving me the space to keep going, even when it meant it took time away from us. Your encouragement and faith in me is invaluable. You are my heart and give me the ability to show love on pages because of how you love me, even when I get on your last nerve.

To my daughters—This might be the only part of the book you can read but mommy loves you. Y'all encouraged me to be brave and held me when I cried because things didn't go right.

To my FRIEEEEEENDS and sprinting buddies— Y'all know who you are—I **love** you. Y'all have walked me through every moment of anxiety and disbelief and gave me the verbal smackdown I needed to keep going. This would not exist without you, literally.

To anyone reading this book—thank you for taking the journey with Shanice and Kendrick. This story is no longer mine; it's ours now.

Finally, to anyone who dreams of writing, creating, or building something that they see in their dreams, or carry in their hearts—<u>do that shit</u>. Keep going. You probably won't get it perfect on the first try, but keep going. Just start...if you don't like it, start over.

Live your dreams <3 Rielle